EXTRA CREDITS

Mike Lupica

BALLANTINE BOOKS • NEW YORK

Library of Congress Catalog Card Number: 87-29611

ISBN 0-345-36029-X

This edition published by arrangement with Villard Books, a divi-
sion of Random House, Inc.

Manufactured in the United States of America

First Ballantine Books Edition: September 1990

*For Taylor McKelvy Lupica,
the prettiest girl in every room,
the one who taught me about
love, surrounded me with beauty,
and gave me the courage to change*

My thanks to Bill Baccaglini,
sociologist, friend,
Tar Heel basketball fan

CHAPTER

1

I WAS having another argument with Natalie Ferrare about Fats Domino when the redhead showed up and started everything.

It was suicide that brought the redhead. The radio touched it off with Natalie. "Blueberry Hill" came on at the end of the *Imus in the Morning* show on WNBC and I told her, sweet as could be, Shut up or die.

She gave me a look like I should be stripped and sold for parts.

"This used to be Richie's favorite song on *Happy Days*," she said. "And you can check me on this, but I think it was Mamie Eisenhower's favorite, too. It was make-out music for her and Ike."

She nodded smugly in my direction. It meant, Your move.

"You were born after 1960," I said evenly. "No one your age understands Fats Domino. Or convertibles, for that matter . . ."

". . . or Willie Mays," she finished wearily. "Or drive-in movies, a lost part of Americana. I know this routine the way cops know Miranda."

We were in my office at Channel A, doing coffee and

bagels and Monday morning newspapers. Natalie had her chair tipped back against my new Ted Williams poster. I'd found it in a Quincy Market print shop when I'd gone up to Boston for the Red Sox home opener. The Kid was in the Sox clubhouse, wearing only a towel and a flinty grin. He looked lean and dark and immortal. Natalie, when invited in for its ceremonial hanging, said it looked like the test cover for a new magazine: *The Sluggers of Chippendale's*.

Now she was pointing at me with her cigarette, saying, "You're not going to go off on one of your riffs now about Freddie (Boom Boom) Cannon, are you? Because if you do, I'm out of here."

I said, "You love rock and roll. Fats Domino is what rock and roll is supposed to be about. It's not all those guys with their marathon runners bodies and tight pants and eyeshadow. It's guys like Fats, and Chuck Berry, guys who've been on the road their whole lives, playing kind of music. You like the Rolling Stones, right?"

Natalie said, "I did until Mick's lips were bigger than Mick."

"Well, you know whose records the Stones listened to when they were starting out?"

"Connie Francis's?"

"They listened to Fats. They listened to 'Ain't That a Shame' and 'I'm Walkin' and 'Blueberry Hill' and 'Blue Monday.' It was Fats who showed Mick it was okay to bury vocals under the instrumentals."

Sarcastically, Natalie said, "Hold the *phone*." She smiled, carefully tipped her chair forward, grabbed her coffee cup off the floor, sipped, leaned back.

"Natalie, when I was growing up, Fats wasn't on top anymore, but anybody who knew anything about music knew he was still cool. Fine. Real goods. The way Ray Charles is real goods."

"When you were growing up? When you were growing up, there were only two Lennon Sisters."

Marty Pearl, my cameraman, sidekick, best friend, was on the couch. I saw he was shaking his head sadly, side to side.

"You feed her straight lines like that, she'll make you feel older than argyle."

He was right, but I stayed with her.

"Fats had twenty-one gold records when rock and roll was young. They used to line up at the Brooklyn Paramount at eight in the morning for him back in the fifties for those shows Alan Freed used to put on. Bums like Pat Boone kept trying to knock off his stuff, and Fats didn't mind. He was just out there on the road, playing his music."

She made the move again with her chair, grabbing her bagel this time. It was cinnamon and raisin, which I felt was vaguely anti-Semitic.

"Let's wrap this up," she said. "So what you're saying is, you'd rather listen to Fats than The Cars?"

I ignored her.

She said, "ZZ Top?"

I looked over at Marty. He was reading the personals from the *Voice*.

"You're not going to help?"

"I can help you," he said, "only if you happen to be looking for a quote WF, thirtyish, who likes walks in the park, candlelit dinners at out-of-the-way French restaurants, California whites, androgynous role playing, semipublic sex and occasional costumes unquote."

Natalie shot him a disgusted look with a quick turn of the head. "You made up the last part."

"Did not," Marty said in a mock whine. "Did not, did not, did not." And offered her the *Voice* as evidence.

I said, "Anyway, and in summation, you can make fun of Fats all you want. But he will always be near the top of any Finley List that includes great things in life, all time."

He would. He was solidly in the middle of the pack, with Earl Monroe, the Adidas Country sneaker, the VCR, *Maverick* reruns, *Singin' in the Rain*, the Final Four of collegiate basketball. Right after the Red Sox, Benny Goodman, Cagney and Astaire. Spencer Tracy.

Jeannie Bogardus Finley, wife, was a whole different list altogether. Jeannie was beyond category. Problem was, she was currently beyond category with the East Africa Safari

Company, touring Kenya for her magazine, *Era*. I hadn't wanted her to go, the way I hadn't wanted to go to Vietnam.

I've never been to Africa, she said, and you said you'd never take me.

But you have to get shots, I said. You hate shots.

No, she said. *You* hate shots.

They shoot deserters in the army, I said.

She said, I'm going, bub.

She went. As usual when she went farther than the Midtown Tunnel, I felt like someone had rearranged the furniture in my life.

I was also off-line because of a trip Natalie herself was taking to Los Angeles the next day. She was to meet with the general manager of KCBS, the CBS owned-and-operated station out there. He wanted to talk to her about becoming a general assignment reporter. On the air. Out there. If the interview went well, Natalie was going to stay for a six-week tryout while we were in reruns.

"I'm bringing the big suitcase," she said when she told me about the offer. "The interview *will* go well, of course."

"Of course," I said. "Ferrare of Rodeo Drive. Breaking the big ones from Giorgio's to Bijan. Credit card trouble is her business."

Truth of the matter was, I was worried about her. I always knew she'd go onward and upward, she had all the goods, any fool could see that, but I thought New York was better for her, I thought she needed a little more groom time with P. Finley.

And bull.

Shit.

The real truth of the matter was this: Natalie was my right hand, pure and simple, and I knew I wasn't going to find anyone remotely like her anytime soon, if ever, even if I would have had to be tortured to tell her any of that.

I looked at her across the office. She had grabbed all the *Times* from Marty's lap. The black hair was long and scattered, thicker and a little stiff-looking that spring, like three different guys named Bruce had cut it. She had finally given in to some tortoiseshell reading glasses; they looked terrific.

In early June she had a coffee-bean tan already. The jersey was white, with huge dots of various colors scattered all over it in some incomprehensible—to me—high fashion way. Young woman from Vassar. Channel A was just the overture. We all knew it, me and her and Marty.

Now the goddamned general manager from KCBS knew it too.

To top it off, cherry on the whipped cream, I was trying to quit smoking. It was fifty-two days since my last Marlboro. It was only like Martina giving up Wimbledon.

As Natalie read the newspaper, of course, she was exhaling more smoke than a bus. So I said, "You're being an awfully big help in my campaign to scrub-brush the lungs."

She looked up. Her reading glasses slipped down to the end of her nose. "Think of it this way. I'm not down there on the field with you. But I'm rooting my heart out. I mean that."

She folded the *Times*, careful not to let it touch her outfit. The *Times* is all the news that's fit to print, but it can make you dirtier than a pig.

She said, "Besides, you're not cranky because of nicotine withdrawal. You're cranky because Jeannie is there and you are here."

"By George, I think she's got it," Marty said in his best 'enry 'iggins.

I sighed theatrically.

"Where could a man such as myself—a simple man, a decent man—ever hope to find a stronger support system than the two of you?"

"The Y?" Natalie said.

Delores buzzed then. I hit the intercom switch.

"Second place, American League East." It was where the Red Sox were. But the Milwaukee Brewers, two months into the season, were already six games ahead. Who knew about the Brewers?

"Someone to see you, white hope." Delores was black, round, cute, divorced, mother of two, funny and indispensable. Marty's theory was that she'd run away from the other Cosby kids.

I said, "State your business, woman."

"Business *is* a woman. Young one, honey. From Washington Square University. Says her name is Lea Ballard. Lea spelled L-E-A. You spoke at her class 'bout a month ago. You said if she ever needed anything, come by. Says she's come by, here she is, could she see you."

I always told college kids that, but no one had ever stopped by before, which is why I kept telling college kids that.

Washington Square University, known as The Square to students and faculty, was my alma mater. It was located downtown at the end of Fifth, and surrounded Washington Square Park. Once a year, sometimes twice, I went back to The Square and spoke to one of the television classes at the new Goldman School of Communications.

I said to the intercom, "She standing right there?"

"Not close enough to hear."

"Got any idea what she wants?"

"Just said she needed to talk to you, great Peter Finley, trouble fixer, finder out of things."

"So send her in," I said and sighed. A college kid with a problem. Or needing a job. Either way, it seemed like a perfect addition to the rest of my day. I started to reach into my shirt pocket for the red-and-white pack of Marlboros that had been sitting there since freshman year at The Square, when O'Rourke taught me how to smoke.

Natalie grinned, patted her own heart, said, "I know, it gets me right here too."

She and Marty stood up, as if on cue. His denim shirt, I noticed, actually looked new. Not so the chinos. The big man said, "We'll talk about the reruns when you finish being a class outing." He meant *The Finley Report*. It was our twice-a-month *60 Minutes* turn on Channel A, *60 Minutes* only sassier, and almost always about New York City, unless a pope died. It had my name on it because I stood in front of the camera. But Marty and Natalie and Dwan Bagley, now my full-time editor, did most of the heavy lifting, which was why when I got awards, they did.

My motto was, presentation is everything.

At the door, Natalie turned and said, "Fats Domino is just an old boner."

I said, "Boner? Fats? Do you know what a boner is?"

"Marty said I was probably too young to know, but you would." She curtsied for a finish. "You're an antique, Finley. Come to grips with it."

THERE are redheads and redheads. They are too perky or have too many freckles or their faces are redder than their hair or they look a little too much like Raggedy Ann.

Lea Ballard was Maureen O'Hara.

When she came through the door I wanted to say, "I always loved you with the Duke."

I remembered her now from the class, a senior thing about local television news. She was a stunner. You don't see a lot of red hair that falls into the mane category. Lea Ballard had it. It went to her shoulders and was thick and had some wave to it, but not too much wave. The skin was cream, no other way to describe it. Eyes green. She was somewhere between five feet tall and six, but she seemed to play bigger, as they said in basketball. The clothes were simple—men's tattersall shirt, white jeans, tight—but she made them look rich the way Jeannie could. The clothes held the curves fine.

I thought: I must help this woman. A mind is a terrible thing to waste.

I came around the desk, shook hands with her, helped her into her chair, said, "Before you say anything, it's Peter. Not Pete. Not Mr. Finley. Especially not Mr. Finley. I already

8

have an assistant, named Natalie, who takes an uncommon glee in my personal aging process.''

She said, "What year did you get out of The Square?''

"I mean it, don't start with me, punk.''

She seemed to relax her grip on the sides of the chair and laugh a little bit with her eyes. She took the hands and folded them in her lap. I gestured at her with my coffee cup. A shake of the head, no, thanks. I sipped some coffee. It didn't taste very hot, or very good. Only the first couple of sips do. After that, it's just you and the caffeine.

I smiled. WNBC was still playing softly. I could hear "Rockin' Robin." I wondered if Lea, or Natalie, cared why I had always thought "Rockin' Robin" was such an underrated song.

Lea looked at the Ted Williams poster.

"I've got Yaz in my room at The Square.''

"You're kidding? Red Sox fan?''

"I'm from Wellesley,'' she said, relaxing a bit more in the chair with the subject, and the common ground. "Only child. You know, son that wasn't, and all that? My dad lives and dies with the Sox. As far back as I can remember, he's had season tickets at Fenway.''

I said, "When I was a kid, bleacher seats cost a dollar.''

"I never, you know . . . could you see from out there?''

"The ushers brought updates.'' I leaned back and put my new Countrys up on the desk. They were very white, the stripes very green.

"Okay,'' I said. "We've established a practically impeccable value system. You're from Boston, you're a Sox fan, you go to The Square, you want to be in television news. You do want to be in television news, right?''

"Yes.'' She reached into her striped canvas bag that said "Gap'' near the zipper, took out a pack of Kent III's and lit one with an orange Bic lighter.

Wasn't anyone paying attention to the Surgeon Fucking General?

I said, "So what can I do for you?''

Lea Ballard said, "I think someone killed the girl who lived down the hall from me.'' She wanted it to come out more dramatic. But she tried too hard, so it sounded like a line from a school play.

"As in homicide, that sort of killed?"

She uncrossed her legs, leaned forward in the chair. Maybe it wasn't going the way she had rehearsed it in the cab uptown, or the bus, or subway. I noticed her eyes were a little too far apart, like Jackie O's. You had to look at one, then the other.

"Not homicide technically," she said. "Of course Julie pulled the trigger herself. But I'm sure somebody drove her to it, and for me, it's the same as if they killed her."

I happened to know what she was talking about.

A month before, Friday night as I recalled, a Washington Square coed had walked into the middle of Washington Square Park, less than fifty yards from the police cruiser that is always there day and night, took off her raincoat, showed the dope dealers and guitar players and various street people that she was dressed only in bra and panties, and shot herself dead through the head. Jeannie and I were in the Bridgehampton house at the time, in the middle of a two-week vacation before her safari. I followed the story for the three or four grisly days it lasted in the New York papers.

The *Post*, the paper that belongs at supermarket checkout stands, had taken the details and run all the way down the field with them.

For the *Post*, a suicide in bra and panties was rare meat for a hungry old dog.

"Lea," I said, "if it's the one in the park, it's not like the circumstances were mysterious or anything. There was a park full of witnesses, even if most of them were probably doped up to a fare-thee-well. It's a horrible story. I'm sorry she was your friend. But she just pulled the trigger and got it over with. Julie, you said her name was?"

"Julie Samson. Twenty-one years old. From Pound Ridge. You know? Northern Westchester, practically right on the New York-Connecticut line?"

I told her I knew where it was. The Bridgehampton traffic was making the trip longer and longer. Jeannie and I had looked at some houses in Pound Ridge.

I said, "Was she a close friend?"

She had walked over to the window and stared out at West Fifty-seventh. Now she came back and sat down. There was one drag left in the cigarette, she took it.

"Close? Not hang-around close, or shop-with close or the kind of close where you share secrets about guys. We had some classes together sophomore and junior years. Not this year, but she was a senior too. I liked her. I thought she was pretty in all the right ways, as shy and nervous as she was. I'm sure she didn't think of herself as pretty. But she was. Maybe it made her prettier, her not knowing. Anyway, she wasn't the type to do anything in a big, showy way. Even kill herself. Somebody, or something, did something really awful to her. She was pushed. Bra and panties? Good God."

"It's the way it usually is with suicide," I said gently. "They end up, they feel like they're getting pushed by the ocean."

"No, dammit!" She snapped it. Then she looked away, shrug of the red hair, as if startled by the sound of her own voice in the office. When she spoke again, the bite was out of her voice.

"I'm sorry, but you sounded like a cop there. For them it was open and shut. There was an autopsy, a routine investigation. You know, they treat suicide like homicide, the police."

I nodded. My daddy, Andrew Jackson Finley, known as Jack, had been a homicide major for the Boston Police Department.

"Anyway," she continued, "once they found out there were no traces of drugs in her system—cocaine or crack is what they basically want to find, heroin if they get lucky—and found out she left no note, they closed the book. Julie Samson. Liberal arts major. Rich kid. Her daddy is an advertising biggie on the go. Arthur Samson. You might have read about him recently. He's up for some big appointment from the mayor, to be a commissioner of this new department that will handle all commercials and public relations and promotions for New York City. Julie used to joke that she was majoring in marrying well just to suit him. Her mom is dead. And when Julie made herself dead, the quotes from friends at school and from teachers were all predictable. 'She seemed fine the last time I saw her.' And, 'There was no indication that anything was bothering her that I could see.' And, 'Such a sweet girl.' Pap and crap. And I don't believe it. She was involved in something that made her so crazy she had to kill herself, and somebody somewhere has to know. There is some sonofabitch who as good as did this to her.''

She stuck out her jaw, looked me in the eye, and said: ''It's why I've started conducting an investigation of my own. And why I think I need help from someone like you.''

I fought back a smile, because serious business was being discussed. My problem is life always seems funny as hell to me when it is serious as hell.

And vice versa.

Lea Ballard had moxie. She had shown it just by coming to see me. She was angry. And she had a story to tell.

I said, ''Okay, kid. Tell me what you got.''

I am a legendary pushover.

CHAPTER
3

I STARTED to buzz Delores, by reflex, to tell her to send Natalie back in to take notes. But Natalie was going west, and I was on my own, even with the detail things. I pulled a yellow legal pad out of the middle drawer.

You hear about Finley?

What?

Still takes his own notes.

No shit? Man's an animal.

Lea Ballard was saying, "For one thing, Julie's roommate left school in March. Three months before graduation."

"Name, please."

"Sara Hildreth."

I wrote the name down. She said, "You don't need to write this stuff down."

"Humor me. I take notes once in a while, I still feel like Johnny Deadline, reporter."

She said, "You started out in newspapers, didn't you?" She made newspapers sound like a quaint notion. Milk bottles on the porch.

"How do you feel about Fats Domino and Chuck Berry?"

She said, "What?"

"Never mind. Sara Hildreth, why'd she leave school so suddenly?"

"No one knows. At least no one I've talked to so far. Maybe Julie knew. Maybe Sara knows what was up with Julie." She shrugged. I shrugged back at her. She smiled fully then for the first time since she'd come through the door. It was a beauty, right out of the wrapper. I thought, College seniors. God could still make the living daylights out of them.

"You have any idea where Sara went? She go home? You try to reach her yet? Where does she live?"

"She's from Douglaston, out in Queens. School says her parents are dead. I called the number they had for her in information, got her answering phone. She said on the tape I could leave a message or call Patrick's Pub if it was important. Patrick's Pub turns out to be this Douglaston sort of bar and restaurant where she's working. I called her, said, 'Hi, Sara, it's Lea Ballard.' She hung up on me. Same sunny-disposition Sara as always."

"She tough?"

"Brassy, ballsy, take your pick. I don't like her."

"You try to follow up, go out there and see her?"

"Mr. Finley." She stopped and giggled nervously. "Peter. I said I've started conducting an investigation of my own. I'm also getting ready for finals. See, if Mr. and Mrs. Ballard's daughter graduates on time, and with honors, she can get on with the business of being Jane Pauley. So, no, I haven't been out to Douglaston yet. I went to Pound Ridge for the funeral, but I wasn't in a snooping mode yet. But you've got to admit, it *is* rather an interesting coincidence that one goes, the other dies, within the space of a couple of months."

I said, "The cops must have at least made a pass of checking out the roommate. Maybe I'll make a couple of calls, see what they've got."

I walked over to my new Mr. Coffee, poured more coffee into my cup. I had the jumps, but I kept going. It was something to do instead of smoking.

And if I smoked, Jeannie would know. I had visions of a smoke alarm sounding all over Kenya soon as I lit up.

"What else?" I said to Lea Ballard.

What else: Julie Samson had a boyfriend. Name of Michael Scalia. I wrote it down. According to Lea, Scalia was a student at The Square, but not a fanatic about it, fading into college, fading out. Sometimes he went to class, sometimes he didn't. He was a junior, a year behind Julie Samson, and a city kid. As far as Lea knew, the police had questioned him. But he hadn't shown up for the funeral. It was just one more thing that made Lea want to look into the whole business.

She did not think Michael Scalia was a Cub Scout.

"He looks like he belongs as the second lead in an Italian movie," she said. "Lots of subtitles. You know what he is? Oily is what he is."

I said, "Oily. Where is he now?"

"He's supposed to have an apartment down here somewhere. I remember Julie telling me that once, in passing. I forget how it came up. But the Office of the Registrar doesn't have the address. As far as they're concerned, he's dropped out of school. He's got an attendance record like a dead person. I think he dropped every class except one. When I asked the woman for his transcript, she handed it over like she didn't care. If he was still a regulation student, I would have had to steal it. Anyway, I can't find him. There's a listing in the phone book for an M. Scalia, but no address, and that number has been disconnected. I called directory assistance to see if he had a new number, they said he did, but it's unlisted."

I said, "I'll get it."

"I thought unlisted numbers were impossible to get, you know, by civilians." Then she turned her head a bit to the right and dipped it, like she hadn't heard me correctly. She was wearing diamond earrings, I noticed. They did not appear to have come from the Sears Roebuck catalogue.

"You just said you'd get it," Lea Ballard said. "Are you saying you're interested enough in Julie Samson so you'll help me?"

I said, "No, I'm interested enough in Julie Samson so that you're going to help me."

She started to say something. I held up a hand.

"Easy, I'm going to explain. We are about to go into two months of reruns on *The Finley Report*. It's in my contract. But I hate reruns. And I have the option of doing first-run shows in June and July if I so desire. I happen to so desire right now, because I was unhappy with the last couple of shows we did in May. One was about rent-controlled apartments. I ended up liking Donald Trump, who was trying to kick out the renters, better than the renters. Bunch of screaming yuppies. Scruppies, I call them. Anyway, the show sucked eggs."

It was the caffeine yabbering on.

"When I was a kid, I was always the kind who couldn't leave the basketball court until I made one more long one, swished a bomb like Mr. Larry Bird himself. You getting this? The rent-control show clanged off the front of the rim. The basketball expression is brick. When I fire up a brick on my very own show, I get irritable. Now factor in a couple of more things. My wife is in Africa. Natalie Ferrare, my assistant, is about to go Hollywood on me. I'm available, is what I'm saying. You obviously feel very strongly about Julie Samson. So I'll head down to the old alma mater and see what the hell is going on. If it's nothing, I'll go to the beach. If it's something, I'll need someone to do legwork. You interested, even with finals coming up?"

She put her right hand across the desk, palm up. "You want to cut each other and be blood brothers, or can we just shake on it?"

I said, "Don't feel like you have to try to be snappier than the star." We shook.

I buzzed Delores and asked her if it wasn't too much trouble, could she send Marty back in.

"Soon as I finish my damn *cruller*," came the reply. "And don't be keepin' your finger that long on that buzzer, or I'm gonna go around this office, start tellin' people things I know on you."

White women, black women, old, young, single, married, it's never mattered, none of them have any problems with me at all.

BEFORE she left, Lea Ballard told me Julie Samson had been beaten up in February, not long after everybody came back to The Square for second semester.

"She came knocking on my door about two o'clock in the morning. Said Sara was out. One eye was closed, she had a fat lip, her dress was torn. It was a black thing, elegant as hell, now that I think of it. Anyway, my dorm room isn't exactly Columbia Presbyterian, but I did the best I could to help fix her up. She said she'd been mugged coming home from a party uptown."

I said, "You believe her?"

"You interrupt a lot, you know? I'm getting there. Julie said she'd gotten out of a cab at Fourteenth and Fifth, she wanted to walk the rest of the way, it was such a nice night, not too cold for some reason, et cetera, et cetera, and that was when the two guys grabbed her, but finally she managed to scream and they ran away. Well I said, 'I'm calling the goddamned police.' She practically shrieked at me to put the phone down, that she just wanted to go to bed and forget about the whole thing. She was right there on hysterical. She said she had some bourbon in her room, I went and got it for

her. And as she was leaving, I noticed something I thought
was funny. She had her purse still. I asked her why. She
looked down at it, like she's surprised to see it, and said,
'They threw it back at me after they emptied it.' I thought,
how about that, muggers with a neatness fetish. But I let it
go. The next morning, I saw her walking across the park, I
was on my way to class. And here comes the weirdest part
of the salad: Julie gave me a dodge like nothing had happened the night before. When I tried to talk to her, she bolted
like I was going to mug her or something.''

I said, "Um," and wrote down "Feb mug" on the yellow
legal pad underneath Michael Scalia's name, which was underneath Sara Hildreth's name. Above all that, circled a couple of times, was "Mr. Sam, Pound Ridge," for Julie
Samson's father.

There were lots of question marks next to Sara Hildreth's
name.

The scribbling didn't look like much, but then it never did.
It was just that when there was a rookie around, I got very
busy.

I INVENTED a salary, told Lea that's what interns made at
Channel A. She said she would work for free. I passed along
something Jimmy Breslin, the columnist, told me once when
I said I would work newspapers for free:

"This isn't the Lawn Tennis Association. You don't play
for the love of the fucking game.''

"Gee, I've got it memorized already," Lea Ballard said,
then left.

I went looking for Natalie. I wanted to goose her with the
notion of Lea Ballard replacing her, even for a little while.
Let her think about that on the noon American. Finley, master psychologist. But Ace Brandt, one of the stage managers
for news, told me Natalie had left word she was shopping.

Channel A kept trying to upscale itself with upscale people, but Ace was cool, the way Marty was cool. He looked
like a trucker, as usual. He wore a CAT cap and black T-shirt
and faded denims and boots. Some straw hair escaped from
the front of the cap, which was red. Ace moved his jaw

around so he could rearrange his smokeless tobacco, permanently lodged somewhere between cheek and gum. When he was done he grinned and said, "Yeah, Nat's shopping. Think we ought to cut into the afternoon movie with a bulletin like that?"

"Ace, she's gonna have to get the job in Los Angeles just to pay for the clothes she bought to get the damn job in Los Angeles."

He gave me a low two on that one. The low two had replaced the high five that spring in sports.

Marty was in Charlie Davidson's office. He was tossing a Nerf basketball at a basket attached to the wall near Charlie's file cabinet. The ball is rubber and soft, about the size of an orange and the same color.

I said, "I'm sure this is how it was in London during the blitz. The CBS radio boys going two-on-two. Murrow and Collingwood Nerfing it out with Cronkite and Trout."

Charlie Davidson had hired me at Channel A. He had just been promoted from news director to general manager slash news director. He was a little bigger than Dr. Ruth, and a pip. He was wearing his Charlie uniform: blue button-down shirt, monogrammed. Red suspenders. Red bow tie. Gray slacks. Chain from pocket watch visible out of the pocket of gray slacks. He was trying to get one of his Dr. Grabow pipes lit.

"I thought we were quitting tobacco together," I said. "Is there nothing left in this world for me to count on, nothing?"

Marty tossed a ball in underhanded and said, "It takes a big man to admit how weak he is."

I said, "Or little, in Charlie's case."

Charlie looked up, bored, and said, "Short material? You guys are going to do short material on a Monday?"

A puff of smoke and some tobacco came out of the bowl.

"You pick out the rest of the reruns yet?" Charlie said. He was staring out the window but the question was for me.

I lied. "Yes." He said, "You do the new openings and the updates for the end?" I gave him another nod for yes, a lie to bring up the rear. It was a variation of the game I played with cops.

He had his pipe going now. Charlie was a beauty when it came to smoking. He would hunt all over five boroughs for just the right blend of tobacco, pay anything, but he stuck to his Dr. Grabows. It was why he had the pocket watch, the old Underwood on his desk, the suspenders. Charlie liked what worked.

"So?" he said.

"So there's maybe a chance I'm going to be working on a first-run the next couple of weeks—nothing solid—and I wanted to let you know in case it pans out, because you are the grand fafoo around here."

"I assume you know you make the same amount of money from this company whether you work the next month or not?"

I said, "Charlie, I've read my contract. It came with Bazooka bubble gum, remember? I was shocked it didn't have cartoons of Nancy and Sluggo."

He made nice, peaceful sucking noises with the pipe. "What do you want to work on that's so hot it keeps you away from Bridgehampton?"

I gave Julie Samson to him notebook-style. When I finished he said, "You think there's more to this girl's death than meets the proverbial eye?"

"Yes sir."

Elf smile. "Of course you do." Charlie flicked some tobacco off the front of his shirt and the finger made a big noise against all the starch.

I said, "Oh, and Charlie. I'm going to use this Ballard kid since Natalie is going to be away. I think perhaps she was born with our kind of moves. You know, head fake and down the sidelines. I might have told her we'd pay our intern wages."

"We don't have intern wages. And there is an excellent reason for this. We don't have *interns.*"

"I know. Come up with something. Be a boss."

Marty said, "Dare to be great." I looked at him and grinned. He made being Marty seem very easy. Everybody else sweated to be who they thought they were supposed to be and Marty was never even out of breath. He was wearing a navy blue baseball cap with a red Kansas University Jayhawk on the front.

"You worried about this Natalie business in L.A.?" From Charlie.

"I am and I'm not," I said. "She wants to be a star, she's wanted to be a star since the third grade, but I'm not sure if you took Natalie away from New York she'd be Natalie."

"Let's just hope she examines her conscience and discovers the needs we think she has," Charlie said dryly. "And where are you going to start on this Samson thing?"

"With the dead girl's father. Then the roommate. I want to know why this Sara Hildreth got off the school bus before it stopped moving. Then I'll just wander down to Washington Square University, see what happens. I don't know, it's funny, but I've had college in my head lately. So here comes this thing. Maybe it was drugs, even if she didn't have any in her system. Eventually I'll talk to Michael Scalia, boyfriend, make sure he's brushing after every meal."

Charlie said, "Tell this Ballard girl to stop by sometime this week, I'll give her forms to fill out, if I can find forms." He absently played with the stack of newspapers to his right on the desk. His reading glasses were fixed to a string around his neck; he got them in place on his nose. Charlie read more newspapers than I did in the morning. He had all the New York dailies, plus the *Washington Post, Boston Globe*, the Hollywood trades, when they were fresh. *The Wall Street Journal*.

He had been brought up in newspapers, same as me. He'd won the Pulitzer in Baltimore for editorial writing. Charlie could see it with his own eyes, not be sure it happened until he read it in the papers the next morning. Didn't matter what it was. Natalie didn't think that way, I'm sure Lea Ballard didn't either. Children of television, all the way. Charlie was the dinosaur, I was the trainee. Out of nowhere he came back to Natalie. "Nobody's going to bullshit this girl. She'll go, she'll like it or she won't, then she'll make up her own mind. By herself. Natalie you can't muscle. She goes her own way."

Then nobody said anything while Marty kept flipping the

ball at the basket, hitting half his shots. Monday was usually quiet in Charlie's office until the editorial meeting in the afternoon. He mostly read the papers and waited for *Ryan's Hope* to come on television; it was his one soap. "I got the hots for this Mrs. Ryan," he said one day in explanation when I didn't knock and caught him watching during his lunch break.

"And I'll tell you one last goddamned thing about Miss Natalie Ferrare, while we're practically on the subject," Charlie said. He snapped shut the Sports Monday section of the *Times* like it was a briefcase. "If she comes back here and says she's leaving and I can't give her a big enough job to keep her, we're planting a pound of prime dope in her apartment and getting her sent to women's prison until she comes to her senses."

"Give her hell," Marty said, and walked out the door. I was right behind him.

I TOLD Delores to book studio time for Thursday or Friday, on the chance that I goosed myself into doing the new openings. And I told her to book a limousine to take Natalie to Kennedy. We were at her desk. She grumped and put down the *TV Guide* crossword. She was wearing a plum-colored pantsuit, silver earrings and eye shadow the color of the pantsuit. Delores had lost thirty pounds in the last six months. It was why she was so feisty with me again. She was feeling good about herself.

She said, "Long one or short one?"

"I beg your pardon."

"You want one of them little town car homo limos, or a stretch?"

"Stretch. You've become quite a fox, you know that, Delores? You make Diana Ross look like she's been beat up."

"You're right," she said. "But I'll tell you one thing for sure: This girl is gettin' awful sick a *chicken*."

I said, "Also tell Miss Ferrare when she comes back from shopping that she is not to leave town without stopping by my apartment tonight, even for five minutes." Charlie and

Marty and I were doing boys' night in, pizza optional, for Red Sox vs. Indians, Monday night game on ABC.

"Done," she said. "Now could you please tell me where you're goin' when you should be doin' those openings Charlie made me check on, sayin' you didn't do them like you said you did, he knew it, don't lie for you like I always do?"

I thought, The frightening thing is, I always understand her.

"I'm going down to Washington Square University and meander about."

She opened *TV Guide* back up and found the crossword.

"Never been anyone who could meander like you," she said, and frowned at the crossword. "But before you go: What's that little midget bandleader's name on Letterman?"

I GOT out of the cab at Fourteenth Street and walked into all the wonderful hurly-burly of lower Fifth Avenue, the perfect mess between Fourteenth and Washington Square Park, which still had the arch at the north entrance. It looked the same as it had the spring of my junior year at South Boston High, when Jack Finley brought me to New York to see The Square.

That day we had walked all the way downtown from Forty-second. It was my first visit to New York City; up to then New York had been movies and television shows, mostly cop shows, and *New York* magazine and all the papers I could get my hands on at The Out of Town Newsstand in Harvard Square.

And that silly old arch, connected to nothing on either side, sold me. Other people got greeted by the Statue of Liberty or the Empire State Building from the air, or that first shot of the skyline when you drove in over the Triboro, or approached the Lincoln Tunnel. Good for them. Me? The city, Manhattan, she just sat there at the bottom of Fifth and said, "Here's the door to the rest of your life, boy. You coming, or what? I don't have all day."

And not so much had changed. The big New York changes were uptown changes, skyrise changes, full of noise and traffic, cranes and jackhammers, cement trucks snorting and slopping around like pigs. The Village seemed more content to play the hand it had been dealt, even with the remodeling of Tribeca and SoHo, the yuppie invasion. The Village still presented itself with normal confidence: This is me. . . .

There was Parsons School of Design on the right. The Lone Star Cafe on the left, where I first heard Kinky Friedman and His Texas Jew Boys sing "They Ain't Makin' Jews Like Jesus Anymore." And back on the right: the Forbes Magazine building, a gray suit of a thing, stolid and a little stuffy for the neighborhood. And down a little, still on the right as you walked south, the First Presbyterian Church, dark and somber and a little forbidding, fronted by one of the most elegant, flowered lawns in Manhattan. The eighteenth green at Augusta National didn't get the love the lawn got at First Presbyterian, southwest corner, Twelfth and Fifth. Across from it, down two blocks on the left, was the restaurant One Fifth, where you could get a good meal and listen to crazy ladies, crazy really, with dyed blond hair play the piano and sometimes get up and walk around the room with an accordion. . . .

Then I was passing underneath the arch again and into the park, which always saddened me, because if the street had not changed, the park had. One late uptown night in the past I heard the writer Jack Richardson describe Elaine's in its early days this way: "Just one large permissive room." The park had been that once, the best lawn party in the city. But now it had grown seedy and sad somehow and—worse—old. The dope dealers had no charm and neither did the place. Maybe there had been as many bums on all the benches when O'Rourke and I had shown up as freshmen. But I could not believe it. Maybe the statue of Garibaldi over there was rakish and dashing then, him reaching for his sword like that. Now he just looked like someone else in funny clothes looking to make a buy.

It was a sixties place hanging on in the eighties, silly and shopworn as the Grateful Dead. And it must have been greener, had to be, when O'Rourke and I had stormed into college, just full of it. That was when O'Rourke was still convinced that the park had been a potter's field for World

War I soldiers. I explained to him why it couldn't be, but O'Rourke was always tough to move off a notion. Every time we'd see a dog fussing with what looked to be a bone, O'Rourke would jump up, point, yell: "Another Sergeant York!"

Now? There was a sign stuck in the lawn: "Leash Dog, No Dog Litter!!! Fines $15 to $100!" Rates had gone up. I thought, What sort of doggie crime was worth the whole hundred?

There was a Sabrett hot dog stand. ASPCA Mobile Unit. Same old plaza fountain. Across Washington Square South was the Kornheiser Library to the left, and the Wirth Student Center to the right, La Guardia Place separating them. There was another sign next to the concrete petanque—sort of Greek bocce—courts; it read, "Alcoholic Beverages Prohibited." They didn't need the sign. The bums were past caring about misdemeanors, and everybody else was shopping at the best fresh-air drugstore in Manhattan. If you wanted to drink there were bars all over the neighborhood, great ones: Googie's, over on Sullivan, and Chumley's, which had been a speak-easy back in the twenties, and Emelio's, which was Gil's when I was at The Square, and the Paper Moon and the Cedar Tavern, on University Place.

I wanted a cigarette. I walked across to La Guardia Place and through the front door of Wirth, past a whole wall of bulletin boards and then upstairs. O'Rourke and I had attended our first and only mixer at Wirth, first week, freshman year. Mostly it had been used for small concerts: Tom Rush and Laura Nyro, the Kingston Trio, even Judy Collins. I could not remember the girl I took with me to Judy Collins.

I went outside to the terrace and took in the wide-angle view of the park. The clouds were gone, it had turned into a fine spring show-off afternoon. The kids were going home soon. The seniors were going—no shit—Out Into the World. It was goodbye for the summer, or for good. I remembered how O'Rourke and I had come out of Judson Hall the morning after the Commencement Ball, wearing our graduation robes as bathrobes, after maybe an hour of sleep, if that. We had left the Commencement Ball early and gone everywhere the night before, drinking everything, playing "American Pie" on the jukebox a thousand or so times; the jukebox was either at Googie's or Gil's, we had closed one or the other, or both. And in the morning we brought our beers outside, wearing those graduation robes, and smirked while everybody said their solemn farewells. Of course we didn't know then, the two smart asses, playing college wise guys right to the end, that the ceremony *was* solemn, and important. We would have laughed like hell at the thought, O'Rourke and me, but we were watching as everybody said so long to kid stuff. Or it was saying so long to us.

But why did Julie Samson say so long her way?

All the way at the other end of the park I saw a girl, a big blond girl, come swinging through the arch, book bag slung carelessly over her shoulder, the stride good and long, hair bouncing and shining, smiling at the day. Probably a senior who was done. Or maybe a junior who knew she'd be back. I thought of the first time I saw Jeannie Bogardus, two years behind me, freshman to my junior, eat up the park that way, with a couple of girlfriends, like she knew the whole world was giving her the eye, wondering, Who is *that*?

Okay then. I was going to have to find out what spoiled it all for Julie Samson.

CHAPTER

5

THE Red Sox-Indians game was in the seventh, Indians ahead 6–4, when the house phone rang. It was Lenny Morrissey, the ex-boxer who worked as our doorman. Lenny said, "Miss Ferraro on her way up." I knew he meant Natalie. Lenny had been putting the *o* on the end of Natalie's name ever since Geraldine ran for vice president. When Lenny wasn't having trouble with vowels, it was consonants. I think it was just all the other left hands belonging to all the other lightheavies that did it. I told him to send Miss Ferraro up. On the television, Tim McCarver, who was working the game for ABC, said Wade Boggs shouldn't be guarding the line at third. McCarver was the regular announcer for the Mets. I had decided a month after he came to town from Philly I would rather listen to him do a baseball game than eat Oreos.

It was no small thing.

Marty was stretched out in front of the set on the rug, hand holding his head up, Moosehead beer in his other hand. Now he had on an Indians cap, he said, because they had wised up and put the chief back on the front.

Marty said, "You already sprung for the limo. Don't try to hold on to her leg when she leaves."

Charlie got up and walked over to the bar and poured more martini from the pitcher into his glass. "Goodbyes suck," he said, and drank.

Natalie knocked and I went over and let her in. She breezed in and took over. "We ship out in the morning," she said, positioning herself on the arm of Charlie's chair. "I know I don't have to tell you men this is the mission that could turn the whole magilla around." She wore a man's tweed blazer, black baggy slacks, black leather workout sneakers and a blue T-shirt that read, "And on the 8th day, He created the Dallas Cowboys." I marveled again how much she reminded me of Jeannie. She just wasn't as soft as Jeannie, because she didn't know soft was okay yet.

From the floor Marty said, "You're all set, we've stenciled your name into all your undies."

I asked Natalie, "You want a drink?"

"I'm fine. I gotta run in a minute, go meet some people over at Sam's Cafe. You know Sam's Cafe?"

I did. "It's owned by one of the Hemingway actress granddaughters," I said. "Is it the one with the lisp, or without?"

"Without," Natalie said. Everybody watched the game. They came out of a commercial, and Natalie said that McCarver looked like Huey Lewis. Charlie wanted to know how that could be, since Huey Lewis used to be a Black Panther. I sipped some Jack Daniels.

"When's Jeannie coming back exactly?" Natalie said.

"I dunno. She called from Nairobi last week on her way to Tanzania and said she'd call again in six days. She doesn't call tomorrow I'm hiring who's ever still alive on *Wild Kingdom* to go bring her back."

Charlie said to Natalie, "Don't you make up your mind about anything while you're out there." He put his hand up and gently rubbed her back.

"I won't," Natalie said.

Marty sat up and made a sound like a ship's horn by blowing on the top of the empty Moosehead bottle. "Remember," he said. "No matter how funny they are, we're funnier.'' Natalie smiled this sweet young-girl smile at Marty and said, ''I think I've got it. Funnier. That go for Finley too?'' She pulled up the sleeve of the tweed jacket and squinted at her watch. ''Listen,'' she said, ''I've gotta get over to Sam's so some other people can have fun tonight too.''

She looked at me.

''I'm going,'' she said softly. ''Okay?'' Which was softer still.

I got up.

''Okay.''

''This Lea Ballard, she's sharp?''

''Well, sharper,'' I said. ''At least since she got out of that hospital for the criminally insane.''

''Whatever you're starting tomorrow,'' she said, in a voice still a size too small, ''it won't be the same without me, buster.'' She got out of Charlie's chair and came across to me and hugged. I hugged back. ''It will most definitely and assuredly not be the same without you,'' I said into her neck. Then she said, '' 'Night, John-boy.'' It was the play she always made when she thought things were getting out of hand, hokeywise.

I put my arm around her shoulder and walked her to the front door.

''I'll probably hate it,'' she said. ''Los Angeles will win. They'll probably have to stop it on cuts.''

''Probably,'' I said.

Out she went.

MARTY and Charlie wanted to go to O'Rourkes after the game. I told them boys' night in meant in for the distance. They went without me. I had just fixed myself a closedown Jack Daniels when Lea Ballard called with Arthur Samson's home phone number. I wrote it down, then I said, ''Where'd she get the gun? I forgot to ask before.''

''Julie?''

''No, Squeaky Fromme.'' I took a small bite out of the drink.

''No one knows where she got it, as a matter of fact. It

was some kind of twenty-two. But can't you get them almost anyplace, you know, Times Square, in there?''

''Was she the kind to walk into a Times Square anyplace and buy a handgun? And if she did, when? She get it just to use on herself, or did she have it a while?''

''You mean she might have had the gun for another reason?''

I said, ''I was thinking.''

Neither one of us had an answer for that one. I told her I'd call Samson in the morning, see what he said, call her with a plan. Letterman was a rerun, but I watched it anyway, then a rerun of the eleven o'clock news, then the *Sportscenter* wrap-up show on ESPN with all the baseball scores and highlights. I finally went to bed halfway through an old *Dobie Gillis* on the Christian Broadcasting Network, just as Dobie and Maynard G. Krebs were cooking up something for poor Zelda. I'm a real ball of fire when my wife is out of town.

CHAPTER

6

ARTHUR Samson said he was leaving for his office and that it was his first day back since. Neither one of us needed for him to say since what.

"So please make it brief, Mr. Finley," Samson said.

I asked to see him. He said no right off; it came across like a reflex. But before I said anything else he changed his mind. He gave me an address on Third that he said was at Fifty-fifth. The name of the company was Halsey, Dana, Samson and Earl.

Samson said, "I'm really not disposed to do anything on camera with you this morning."

"I understand. Sure. Maybe we can do it down the road someplace, after you see where I'm going with this piece."

"Ten o'clock," he said, and hung up before I could say roger.

Lea met me at Fifty-fifth and Third. The offices were in the semi-skyscraper they'd managed to build around P.J. Clarke's, which was still next door. Michael's Pub was on the ground floor of the building; Woody Allen played jazz clarinet sometimes on Monday nights, and Torme sang there when he was in town. But the block belonged to Clarke's. It wouldn't move, this great part of old New York you couldn't push around. Danny Lavezzo, the bear who owned it, wouldn't be bought out. So a deal was worked out and the red brick saloon was left right where it had always been, on the northeast corner, across from the post office. Like it was an immortal in the monument section at Yankee Stadium.

Lea said, "You hang around much at Clarke's?"

"Let me explain it to you this way," I said. "In my single days, Clarke's was the Kentucky Derby. T.J. Tucker, which is over at Fifty-ninth and First, was the Preakness. And O'Rourkes, bless its heart, was the Belmont Stakes, longest track of the three. But believe me, I could go the mile and a half."

She gave me an odd look, past serious, almost serene. "You drink a lot?"

I said, "Used to."

She said, "Me too." It was a comma more than a period, but before I could ask her to clarify she was a yard ahead of me, moving briskly toward the revolving doors across from Michael's Pub.

The offices for Halsey, Dana, Samson and Earl were on the thirtieth floor. A young man with spiked hair shaded blond and featuring what appeared to be a magenta streak pointed from behind the reception desk and told us Mr. Samson's office was with the other partners, all the way to the back. Then he said he better show us, it was kind of confusing. He stood up and I saw his body was surrounded by a whole wing of khaki from one of those Banana Republics.

"Gender confusion," Lea whispered. When spiked hair got far enough ahead I said, "There seems to be a lot of it going around." Lea grinned and said, "I don't care, I want those slacks."

We took a couple of lefts in a maze of cubicles, a hard right, kept going, changed planes with a tight connection in Chicago, and ended up in another reception area. I decided once again that I would rather be a hockey referee than work anyplace remotely like Halsey, Dana, Samson and Earl.

Spiked hair pointed triumphantly toward Samson's door. He gave my name to Samson's secretary. The nameplate said she was Miss M. Robbins. Miss M. Robbins, the apparent victim of an eyeshadow epidemic, picked up her phone and said, "Mr. Finley and a young lady."

I said to Lea, "It's the advertising concentration camp."

Miss M. Robbins was vigorously nodding her head.

"How many serial killers you think come out of a setup like this?" Lea asked.

Miss M. Robbins kept nodding after she hung up the phone. Samson's door opened automatically, with a big whoosh. We were on. I took another look at Lea. The Tuesday morning outfit was a blue jean skirt, lightweight blue sweater not quite as dark as the skirt, white Keds, ankle socks. I wondered briefly if it was a good idea to have her with me.

Finley: "Um, Mr. Samson, I'm here to talk about your dead daughter." Hook a thumb at Lea, in her Keds and ankle socks. "You remember, she was one of *these*."

Arthur Samson was a corporate bruiser. It was all right there in the way he carried himself. Mr. Gruff. A lot of shoulders. There was a hawklike quality to the face, especially around the nose and eyes; he was probably a rake when he was younger. But he was getting jowly now. The jacket of the beige suit, buttoned, was straining against his belly. I could almost hear the groans. Samson tried to suck in the belly some as he came across the room, meaty hand out. Sucking didn't help. He couldn't make the lines of the beige suit what they were when he bought it, about fifteen pounds ago, I guessed. And I saw some redness around the tip of the nose, and veins here and there, dark blue, running toward his ears. He drank.

He said, "Mr. Finley. I know your work." We shook hands. I said, "Thank you for seeing me, I'm sure this is another drain." He studied me for a couple of beats longer than normal and said, "You're sure." Almost making it into a question. I made a half-turn toward Lea, who said, "Lea Ballard, Mr. Samson. I went to school with Julie." Now he studied her. We were all still bunched about three feet inside his door. The mention of his daughter didn't seem to soften

Arthur Samson any, or back him up. Finally he said, to Lea, "I remember now. You were at the funeral."

"Yes, sir."

"You were a close friend of my daughter's?"

"Not close. I've explained that to Peter. But I liked her very much. There was a sweetness to her. You didn't have to be all that close to see it."

We moved across the room to his desk. Samson sat down and then we did. The window behind him had an uptown view of Third. It was pretty good, if you liked cranes. The morning sun was doing its job; it was actually a lot of sun, bouncing off windows and the cranes and the scrapers already up, toward Bloomingdale's and beyond. It was just another Manhattan angle. I never got tired of finding them. The skyline was getting way too busy, but it was still the best.

The walls of Samson's office were covered with framed print ads of various sizes, presumably representing big accounts for HDS & E: instant soup, a new Japanese camera and VCRs, bicycles, cereal, a home computer, cat food. Some of it looked fine.

The rest of it looked to be the product of minds that couldn't sell clemency on death row.

There wasn't a photograph of Julie Samson anywhere in the room, unless an instant soup or a cat food was hiding it. Or maybe the low-cal beer. Samson sipped coffee out of a heavy-looking brown mug about ready to move into the stein category. Big man, big things.

Where do you start? The man's daughter, only daughter according to Lea, had blown her brains out on date night. You just try the first door you come to, give it a jerk. So I said, "Mr. Samson, when was the last time you spoke to your daughter?"

"A couple of weeks before . . . *before*," he said. "I was leaving for Los Angeles, and I wanted to let her know where I'd be if she needed anything, money or so forth."

"How did she sound?"

The big mug went down, probably harder than he meant. "You mean, was she on the brink, Mr. Finley? Pondering the abyss? Gun to the temple time? No, she was not. She sounded subdued, as always. There was worry in her voice, below the surface, rippling the water, but that was normal. We made some small talk about her getting ready for finals. I asked if she had made any summer plans yet. She said she might stay in the city, get a job here. It was nothing. My daughter and I did not, in the current cliché of choice, connect. But then, that was a common thing." He had been gripping the end of his desk with both hands; now he dropped them into his lap. "I believe I can help you with the next several questions, Mr. Finley. I did not win any Father of the Year awards after my wife died. I probably can't be of as much assistance to you as you thought because I did not know about my daughter's life. So I understand less about her death. When she went off to college, she never really came back. The last few summers were spent in Europe."

Next question, Morley.

"How long ago did your wife die?"

The question surprised him.

"You don't know?"

"I'm sorry."

"My wife died in an automobile accident five years ago. My son, Jonathan, was also killed. My other daughter, Jamie, was in the car. She survived the crash. Physically, anyway. She entered a mental hospital shortly afterward, has been there ever since. The doctors say it's a form of catatonia."

"You think Julie's suicide is related to that in any way?"

"I don't, actually. I asked. The doctors believe Jamie's trauma was induced by being in the car, seeing her mother and brother die before her eyes. I don't really want to go into this, Mr. Finley. I have not had a happy life. I am not *having* a happy life. I would like to ask you to let my daughter rest in peace."

I said, "Lea thinks there were forces at work on Julie, and that we can find out about them. The police tend to close the books on something like this pretty quickly. I go a lot slower."

Samson said, "Forces?" He looked at Lea, at me, back

at Lea. "What do you mean? They told me she wasn't pregnant, or sick."

Lea said, "I just think Julie got mixed up in something she shouldn't have gotten mixed up in."

I studied Samson while he focused himself on Lea. Just the business of conversation was reddening his face, exhausting it. There was hangover all around his eyes, I should have spotted it right away. Samson was counting down toward lunch. He could have a couple of bracers, then be on his way; the afternoon would look better than the morning.

"Do you know Michael Scalia?" I asked.

"I met him once. Julie brought him to the house, she was picking up some clothes. I didn't like him. He seemed much older than my daughter, in that way kids who spend their whole life in the city can seem older. A little too glib. You know the type? He was trying to have more polish than college boys are supposed to have. He was why I thought it was wrong for Julie to go to college in the city. I wanted her to go to Connecticut College, her mother went there. Someplace like that. Bennington, even. College is campuses. I kept telling her that. It's getting away and being *at* college."

"But Julie was adamant about going to The Square?"

"Because I was adamant about her *not* going to The Square. It was going to be romantic, she said. The real world."

Lea said, "Julie seemed to lack self-confidence for someone as pretty as she was, and smart."

"Her whole life," Samson said quietly. "She was like her mother that way. Other ways too, but that way most of all. If you didn't tell her she was beautiful a couple of times a day, it reinforced her belief that she wasn't, never had been. I never understood it, frankly, with her or her mother. What man does, after all? I'm sorry, I was brought up to look at things as they are, deal with the damn reality of things. I have lost my wife, lost all my children. I go on."

He got up to refill the mug. Then he sat back down. Coffee for one. Less of a mess to clean up. I said, "When you spoke to Julie the last time, you said she was subdued. Did she say anything in particular that sounded, I don't know, unusual?"

"She just wanted to know about this appointment from the mayor, to be commissioner of city promotion, how that was going. She said money was fine, and that she was enjoying living alone."

"Did you know Sara Hildreth?"

"No. Just that my daughter lent her money sometimes."

"Julie lent Sara money?"

"It was during the last school year, I can't remember which semester. Three thousand dollars."

"How did you find out?"

"Her bank statements came to me, that's how I found out."

"You noticed a big check to Sara?"

"I called Julie on it. She said Sara needed the money. Wouldn't tell me for what. I exploded, as you might expect. I told her you lend your college roommate twenty dollars, or fifty, but not three thousand dollars. Then she said Sara needed help with a student loan, that she was helping a friend out, and there was nothing I could do about it. My daughter, talking to her father from the *city*, don't you know. It was a person, a voice, I didn't know at all. A stranger. She said if I wanted to shut her off, go ahead, she didn't need my money to be her own person."

"Did you? Shut her off, I mean."

Samson tried to laugh. And some kind of laugh sound seemed to come out of him, but all I saw were the sad red drinker's morning eyes, pink edges bracketing nothing. The first one of the day was getting closer. Maybe he wouldn't wait until noon today. He said, "If I didn't give my daughter money, Mr. Finley, then I wouldn't have been giving her anything at all."

"You didn't think she could support herself?"

"She never had before."

Lea leaned forward, said, "My dad says that if you can understand what goes on between a father and a daughter, there isn't anything in the world you can't understand."

Samson gave her a look like someone had untied him. "I seemed to give her all the things she didn't need. After her mother, Connie, died she grew up at other people's houses. I became Halsey, Dana, Samson and Earl.''

I said, ''When was the last time you saw your daughter?''

He took a breath, let it out. ''After she came to the house with Michael Scalia that time. It was the Christmas season, I don't remember the exact date. We had a row in front of the boy before they left.''

Row. Samson had apparently learned English watching BBC-1.

''What about?''

''She said they wanted to move in together.''

''You didn't want her to.''

Samson gave me a look that tried to drop me.

''I told my daughter she was already supporting one room-mate, how could she support two?''

''But she didn't do it,'' Lea said.

Samson said, ''I never got the chance to ask why.''

Lea said, ''She never came back home?''

Arthur Samson looked at his watch.

''She's coming,'' he said. ''In the boxes the school is sending.''

LEA and I took a cab back to The Square. She said she had a 12:30 class in newswriting. She also said if I wanted, she could meet me after it, about 2:30, because she had a three she wanted to blow off.

''You guys still say 'blow off'?'' I said. We were in front of Wirth. Her class was at Lockhart, on the corner of Washington Square South.

''Yeah,'' Lea said. ''But no groovy, in case you were wondering. No bummed out, nobody relates anymore, and we're never mellow, under any circumstances.''

Across the street, at the south entrance to the park, two kids, one black, one white, seemed to accidentally bump into each other. Before they went their separate ways, the black kid handed the white kid something and the white kid handed the black kid money. I assumed the transaction had nothing to do with Cliff Notes, and started looking around for Geraldo Rivera's van.

I said, "Does anybody collegiate catch a few z's in the late afternoon, right before *The Three Stooges*?"

Her forehead wrinkled up. "Negative."

"When the weather really gets warm, do the guys take off their shirts and cop a few bennies over on the lawn?"

Lea said, "Huh?"

"Bennies. Beneficial rays. The sun. Center of the solar system. The one on the raisin box."

"Hey, when *did* you get out of here?" She found the pack of Kent III's from her purse. "Do you want to meet later?"

"Nah. I'm gonna wander around a little bit, see if I can weasel Julie's transcript record, class schedule, whatever, from the registrar's office. I'd also like to find out if they've completely cleaned out Julie's room, and if I need permission from anybody to see it. What I would like you to start finding out, if you can, is what she might have been doing, where she might have gone, her last few hours."

"Okay."

"You think anybody around here ever taps a keg?"

She looked at me, grinning, and smoked.

I said, "People still get down, though, don't they? They must still get down."

"I'll call you." Lea laughed. "If you hear any language that confuses you, write it down, we'll go over it later." Then she went swinging away toward 12:30, knowing all the new words, whatever they were, and being all the college things I was not.

I yelled after her, "Wait till after the network news if you call. I may be catching some z's."

She waved a hand back over her head. It said, get out of here.

The Stooges? Natalie was right. I *was* old.

I desperately needed to come to grips with that.

CHAPTER

MARTY said, "There's a lot of stuff here."

"Girls have nesting tendencies. They start while we're out playing ball."

He looked at me. "How do you know these things?"

I said, "Oprah."

Marty nodded. "You're right. Her and Donahue know everything."

Marty set the lights down on the floor and the Betacam on Julie Samson's stripped bed. He never knows about the lights until we get to the shoot. If there's enough daylight, he just attaches a blue gel filter over the lens. But those are Marty's problems. When he's happy with the lighting and says "Go," I do that.

We were in Room 608, Weinstein Hall, on University Place. It was known as the party dorm when O'Rourke and I were in school. I wondered if it was still the party dorm. Or if there were such a thing anymore. It had been a co-ed dorm, one of the first, in our day. Now from across the hall, or perhaps up above, I could hear the muted sounds of Bob Seger singing "Main Street." Somebody collegiate had some taste at Weinstein. I did not like a lot of the new rock and

40

roll, but I liked Seger, who'd been Springsteen before Springsteen as far as I was concerned.

I sat down on the bed next to the camera. "You want to help me sort through this stuff before we do the setup?" Marty said sure. There were big cardboard boxes, the kind moving companies give you and you put together yourself, crowded into one corner. The boxes hadn't been sealed yet with tape. There were books in some of the boxes, clothes in more; there were still a lot of clothes hanging in the closet and stacked on shelves. Across from the bed, below an empty cork board, was Julie Samson's desk, with drawers piled on top. Under the desk was another moving box half filled with records and tapes.

Marty sat down on the floor, began taking books out. He seemed to take up half the cluttered room with his cluttered self. He is built like an overweight power forward. I had never asked him his playing weight, just assumed it was between two hundred and three hundred, somewhere near the middle. He says he is six-six, with full red beard, surprisingly young face, eyes the color of aquamarines. He favors painter's pants and Hawaiian shirts. He had red hair on top of his head, but you rarely saw it, because of the caps. He wasn't wearing his Kansas Jayhawks cap now. The new one was green, from the Milwaukee Bucks.

If you stuck a guitar in his hands and put him on the stage with the Grateful Dead, everybody would say, Okay, he's with the band. He was the best friend of my life. Now he said, "What exactly are we looking for here, Skip?" Even his soft voice sounded loud in the dead girl's room. We had done all this before, with different people, different settings, and it was always the same. This was her stuff. We were going through her stuff. She had hung the clothes, arranged the sweaters, neatened shoes and shoe boxes. Stuff. Hers. It was never like this in the movies. I sat down next to him, started through a box of my own.

"I don't know," I said. "Something. Or anything. A clue, Inspector Hound. I want to find something that can tie her into other people, who can then tie into other people. A daily calendar. Phone book. Or address book. Her transcripts will help some, but only with grades and teachers and her schedule. Tomorrow we'll visit her roommate, that Sara Hildreth. Maybe we'll locate a possibly elusive swell named Scalia. Today we just root around, try to get lucky.''

Marty said, ''You ever get tired of all the glitter?'' He blew the dust off a brown paperback that had *Four Short Stories, D.H. Lawrence* written on the front in white letters.

I said, ''And to think we get paid for doing it.'' Marty said, ''We should open a school, so's kids could learn what we know about going through boxes.'' He put D.H. Lawrence on the floor and started a new pile of books.

We went through the boxes. Outside we could hear Weinstein getting louder as people came back from classes. Or exams. There was more music. I did not recognize the songs. There was running on the stairs, whoops of female laughter. The school year was coming to an end, that was the real music of the afternoon. When we were done with the boxes, we went into the closet. Julie liked shoes. There were at least thirty pairs, maybe more, along with about six different colors of running shoes. They were organized into rows. The boxes were behind them.

I took the shoe boxes out and tossed them on the bed. Marty was sitting on the windowsill, smoking the last half of a cigar he'd started sometime during the Passover feast, from the looks of it.

He said, ''You're going to go through her shoes? There's a joke in there somewhere.''

''It's a new angle for a series. Podiatrist by day, private dick by night.''

Marty said, ''Not a criminal anywhere who doesn't tremble when he finds out Dr. Scholl is on the case.''

It was the second-to-last box, a red one that had ''Ferragamo'' written on the side, that had the money in it.

I took out a hundred-dollar bill and showed it to Marty Pearl.

I said, ''Dr. Scholl says, Bingo.''

TEN thousand dollars was sitting in the Ferragamo box.

All in fifties and hundreds. Fifties tied together with a

piece of string, hundreds just stacked. There was also a key. It was not the key to Room 608 Weinstein Hall, because I checked.

After we counted the money we put it back in the box. "I think we can rule out her Christmas Club account," I said.

Marty was tossing the key up in the air and catching it without looking, like George Raft.

He said, "She's got a rich daddy. She's got a checking account of her own. When she wanted to loan her roommate three thousand, she took it out of the checking account. Why do you do that if you've got ten thousand in the closet behind the pumps?"

"Arthur Samson said she wanted to loan Sara Hildreth the money. Whether she did it or not is another matter. That's where hard-nosed investigative reporting comes in."

Marty said, "Oh," and handed me back the key, which I put in my wallet.

The room was getting hot. I opened the window. You could see dust dance through the thick beam of sun that came into the room, like one of those toys with fake snow inside it you're supposed to tip upside down.

"She have a job?" Marty asked.

"Not that Lea or her father mentioned. I would think not."

"They got a lottery on this campus?"

I shook my head.

"Why would she stuff money in a shoe box instead of putting it in the bank?"

I said, "A pathological fear of fluctuating interest rates?"

Marty mashed the stub of the cigar on the outside part of the windowsill and then tossed it.

He said, "She had money that she thought she might need for some unspecified reason that she didn't want anybody to know about. That read right to you?"

"You bet."

"So it's cushion money. Cushion against something, but we don't know what. Is ten thousand enough to get the pressure off?"

"You're just full of questions today, aren't you, Sparky?"

He smiled. It is not a big habit with Marty Pearl, smiling.

But when the smiles come from underneath the caps, they are fine to look at.

"I always get chatty when Natalie's not around," he said. "She never lets me talk."

I said, "Ten thousand is enough to get the pressure off only if that's how much the pressure costs."

Marty lifted up the Bucks cap and scratched a thicket of curly red hair.

"But it must have cost more, because Richard Cory went home one night and put a bullet through his head. Isn't that how the poem goes?"

"Yup."

I reached in and took out the hundred-dollar bill on top. It had some miles on it. "So there was something Julie Samson couldn't buy her way out of with her stash."

Marty nodded. "Or didn't get the chance to buy her way out of."

I said, "You ever feel so full of suppositions they get to be like suppositories?" I went into the bathroom and checked myself out in the mirror. I was wearing what I almost always wear for work: Blue buttoned-down shirt. Knit tie, maroon today. Blue blazer. Blue jeans. Adidas Country sneakers. I knotted the tie, did the undone top button, ran a hand through hair I was wearing very short, went back into the room with Marty, who was setting up the tungsten lights. I said, "Richard Cory was a nice touch, by the way."

"I take it you're going to hold on to the money," he said.

"Natch. Where do you want me?"

"I'm going to sit on the window, you get over there by the boxes, then I'll see exactly how much light I'm going to need. Go ahead and mike yourself up and we'll check the sound in a second."

I thought about what I wanted to say. It would be about college dreams being put to rest in boxes, and a room once filled with college life now looking like something in a warehouse. It was May at The Square, I wanted to talk about that, how May was always the best month. The ones in Weinstein were full of talk about finals and summer vacation and going home. And Julie Samson was just things in boxes now, and the things would go home to Pound Ridge without her.

I figured it would play.

Marty finally decided he liked the looks of the room with just the sunlight coming in. We did the sound check. Right before I started he came over and kicked the Ferragamo box out of the shot.

The big lug is an artist.

WE were finishing when I saw him standing in the doorway.

He said, "Well, hello."

Marty was kneeling by the window, packing up. The Ferragamo box was sitting next to me on the bed. I was glad I had put the top back on. I let it sit there like it wasn't there.

I said, "Hello, yourself."

He was a tall, thin black man, with great cheekbones and perfect ebony skin and close-cropped hair you almost couldn't see. He was wearing a white shirt with dark blue stripes in it, red suspenders, a red print tie, pleated light-gray slacks that were probably part of a suit. He had his hands in the pockets of the pants, and was leaning against the doorframe. I noticed he had an earring, left ear. I thought it made him look more like a king, but a king who had maybe walked through *The Man in the Gray Flannel Suit*.

He finally said, "Can I ask you what you're doing in Miss Julie Samson's room?"

The accent was British, but there was more going on than that. The voice was very deep.

I said, "Didn't you used to be Paul Robeson?"

It got a smile, but not that you could prove it. "Actually, I am the oldest Jackson brother. I chose not to go on the Victory Tour. Messy business that, with Michael and the rest. They cut me completely out of the family. It probably saved my show business career. That said, I must admit we still haven't addressed the issue of who you are, what you're doing here, how you got in, whether or not I should call campus security. Matters such as these." He took his hands, big hands, out of the pockets. Folded his arms across his chest. The only other jewelry besides the earring was a thick silver bracelet around a dark wrist.

I introduced me. I introduced Marty.

"Identification?"

I showed him some. "And who are you?"

"My name is Desmond Akeem Powell. I am an associate professor of African history at this university. I never played basketball. Julie Samson was my friend. I came back from Africa yesterday to find that she was dead. I came over to sit in her room for a while, mourn her in my own way. And now I have found you and Mr. Pearl here. I will come back later."

The manner of speech was clipped and formal. And elegant and altogether well turned out. Like Desmond Akeem Powell.

"My wife is in Tanzania right now, I think," I said.

"I was born in Nairobi. My father was an Englishman born, assistant manager of the Norfolk Hotel. My mother was Kenyan, a teacher of history at university."

I smiled. "Now I know practically everything. Do you play any musical instruments?"

"No, but I have been compared to a clarinet, in appearance, by Julie Samson."

I said, "I'm sorry about Julie. I truly am. I didn't know her. But a girl who did know her has asked me to look into her death. Do you know Lea Ballard? She lives in this building."

"I do not. Again, I have been away for a few weeks. I had only independent study courses this semester, all of which have been completed. Now I am back to teach a course this summer, at the night school. A secretary at Kornheiser told me about Julie. It is a horrible thing. I have met many people at Washington Square University. None as kind or gentle as she."

Marty sat on the windowsill, looking out at the park, smoking a cigar. Desmond Akeem Powell sat on the desk, across from the bed. I leaned sideways, so I was between Desmond Akeem Powell and the box full of money. The closer he got, the bigger he looked. He was Marty's height, with longer legs. Suspenders made him look taller than he was. Suspenders do that. I don't know why. They just do.

"You knew her well, Julie?"

He smiled, following through this time. "On or off the record?"

"When I was a reporter, it only counted if I had the notebook out. Now that I'm one of those sissy television guys, it's only an official at-bat if the camera is rolling."

"Official at-bat is a basketball expression?"

"Baseball. It's off the record, is what I'm saying."

"Fair enough, Mr. Peter Finley. I met Julie last summer in London. I was there to visit my parents. One afternoon, the line was too long at the Hard Rock Café. You know the Hard Rock Café, around the corner from the Inn on the Park?"

I told him I did. Practically in back of the Hotel Inter-Continental. Across the street from Green Park. Or was it St. James Park?, I said.

"Green Park. I was hungry. I started walking up Park Lane, and then a rainstorm hit. I ducked into this little restaurant in the Park Lane Hotel. Julie was seated at the next table. It was such a coincidence, her being from The Square also. We had lunch together, and chatted right through tea. She had four more days in London. We went to the theater each night. One evening, she dined with my parents and myself at a wonderful Italian restaurant off the King's Road, Zianni's. Do you know Zianni's?"

I thought, Desmond Akeem Powell talks like a tour guide. "No."

"Well, the food is quite good, despite the noise."

"Did you and Julie continue seeing each other when school started in the fall?"

"Yes, but only for a short while. She was taking one of my courses, about South Africa. Despite that, I wanted to become more . . . serious with her. She resisted. She said we could only be friends. She did not want to hurt me. I reluctantly acceded to her demands. We remained friends. She did splendidly with the course. But the friendship chilled as the weather did. I would call her sometimes, ask to meet just for a cup of coffee. But she was always busy. Mostly I saw her in the lecture hall."

"Did she ever indicate to you that something was bothering her?"

He rolled his head back. Like his neck was stiff and he was loosening it.

"She didn't have to indicate anything with her words. It was obvious she was not the same girl I had met in the Park Lane Hotel in the summer. The last time we were together was for a drink at the Astor Bar. January, I believe."

"Anything unusual about the day?"

"No, sir. She said she would call, but she never did."

"You remember anything she might have said?"

"We were not together long. I do recall her saying how wonderful it would be to have enough money to travel all the time, so you could always be a stranger, no matter where you were."

"Did you know what that meant?"

"More sadness, do you not think so?"

"You called her after that?"

"A few more times, before giving up. It was not pride, you understand. Just exasperation, and futility."

"And she never said what might be bothering her?"

"No, she never said what."

"Did you know that her roommate had left school?"

"No. You are talking about Sara Hildreth?"

"You knew her?"

Now he moved his head from side to side.

"Enough to dislike her."

I shifted on the bed, saw the box start to tip as the mattress moved, steadied it with my hand.

"Why is that?"

"Do you know her? There is just something not good about her. A hardness that is quite unattractive. She was not good. That is all I care to say."

"You ever have her, Sara, in one of your classes?"

He chuckled. "No, sir."

"Did you know Julie had started seeing a student named Michael Scalia?"

"Michael Scalia?"

"You don't know him?"

"It is a big school, Mr. Peter Finley. Julie told me she was seeing someone, but she never told me his name. If you say it was Michael Scalia, then it was. Did he have something to do with her death?"

"I don't know. Someone did. That's what her friend thinks. We just don't know who, or why. We're just getting started, though. Can I ask you something?"

"I would like to be of help in any way, though I do not understand how."

"Did Julie have some kind of job? She ever mention some kind of job?"

"No. I just assumed her money, what money she had, came from her father."

I said, "I see."

"You will find out why she did such a thing, Mr. Finley?"

"I'm going to try. Would you mind if we talked about a little of what we talked about on camera, as long as we're all here?"

He stood up. "I would rather we didn't mention that Julie and I had dated, if you don't mind. Even innocent as it was, I am faculty at this institution. I am also black. I know Washington Square University is liberal, but I do not want to press the issue."

"You are her friend. I want to talk to her friends." Marty was already unpacking the camera. I said to him, "You have tape left?" He gave me a hurt look, as though I'd insulted one of his caps.

Marty said, "You would have asked Harry James if he had any trumpet left?"

If Desmond Akeem Powell noticed the Ferragamo box, he did not let on. He just stood where Marty told him to stand, answered my questions, talked about the friend who wasn't there when he came back from Africa.

"For seniors, it is the season for joy at this college," he said near the end. "Any college. It is supposed to be both end and beginning, not just end."

I didn't have any questions after that, or anything to add.

I know when my card has been trumped. When we were done, he sat down on the bed, said he would lock up when he left.

I STOPPED by Lea's room at Weinstein. She wasn't back from her 12:30 yet. Or maybe she'd decided not to blow off her three. I slid a note under her door and told her she could meet us at O'Rourkes later, about eight.

Marty said he would drop off the tape at Channel A, then he was going to catch a five o'clock showing of *Deadline USA* at the Bleecker.

"It's the most underrated newspaper movie of all time," he said in explanation. He had parked the van at Fifth Avenue and Tenth Street. Some meter maid terrorist had ignored the press plates and given him a ticket. Marty took it off the windshield, walked down the block, tore it up and threw the remains into a wire basket. He came back and said, "Littering is unlawful."

He got in and buckled up. I leaned through the open window on the passenger side. I said, "Hey, I didn't know you liked newspaper movies."

"Bogie and Ethel Barrymore, man," he said. "Bogie and Ethel Barrymore. Martin Gabel plays a mobster. Bogie's the crusading editor and the paper is dying and Ethel can't save it. Bogie's got the goods on Gabel, though. Gabel tries to threaten him, but Bogie runs the story anyway. He's on the phone with Gabel at the end, down in the room with the presses. He holds out the phone so Gabel can hear. Then Bogie says, 'You hear that, baby? Those are the presses, baby.' The end."

"You've seen the film a couple of times."

Marty said, "I love that scene." He shook his head. "Those are the presses, baby," he said, and drove off.

I had put the money in my leather satchel along with Julie Samson's school records; Jeannie had taken my new correspondent's bag from Banana Republic to Africa with her. I wanted to walk for a while. I stopped in the Barnes and Noble there on lower Fifth and bought the one western by Elmore Leonard I hadn't read yet and a baseball book by E.P. Kinsella, *The Thrill of Grass*. Then I backtracked a little, crossed over to Sixth on Eleventh and went into Balducci's, which is to the word "market" as Fenway Park is to "ballpark." Market doesn't even begin to describe Balducci's, of course. It is bakery, it is deli, it is heaven for a lot of things, but mostly Italian things. I bought a couple of sticks of pepperoni and these mozzarella balls which are dipped in olive oil and pepper and are so wonderful and pungent they will change your political beliefs. There is no afternoon I've ever had that couldn't at least put on new clothes after a trip to a bookstore, almost any bookstore, and a trip to Balducci's. I took Julie Samson's money and the goodies home. The Cubs were playing the Braves on WTBS. Harry Caray had come over to do a couple of innings with his son Skip, who does the Braves games. They are both terrific baseball broadcasters, but the pull of heredity is very strong, because it sounded like a couple of boat whistles having an argument about whether this Dunston kid from the Cubs was going to be a better shortstop than Ozzie Smith. I made a plate of pepperoni and the cheese and some Greek olives, got a bottle of Coors out of the refrigerator, and got ready to camp out on the couch with the provisions until O'Rourkes.

The phone rang in the bottom of the fifth. The Cubs had two on. Andre Dawson was at the plate.

I picked up the phone and caught the caller up on the game. "The Cubs have something going and Andre Dawson is at the plate," I said.

I could hear some snap and crackle and pop. It was either long distance, or someone was calling from the pay phone across the street.

Jeannie Bogardus Finley said, "I've obviously caught you at a bad time. I'll tell the white hunter we've got to wait and see if the Cubs push one across. Catch you after the Masai warriors turn me loose."

I muted the television.

"Come home, please," I said. "I've paid the ransom, I love you, I've been watering the plants."

"I can only talk for three minutes. There are some other

people who have to use this phone." Her voice started to fade. "You're lying about the plants, right?"

"Right!" I was shouting. I felt like I was one of Harry Caray's kids. "How's it going?"

"What?"

"I asked how it's going."

The line cleared up again.

"It's just been your basic life-changing experience, Peter. I'm talking about a beauty so profound you know it will stick to your ribs the rest of your life. It is serene here, and noble, and every day is the sort of adventure that a new day in your life is supposed to be."

It has never been just small talk with Jeannie.

I said, "So if I'm reading you correctly, you're having an okay time?"

I heard her laugh.

"I don't know if I can ever get it down right in words, but I'll tell you what: You're coming back here with me someday, sport."

"I don't think so," I said. Now the line was breaking up every couple of seconds. I was hearing my own words in echo. But nothing has ever stopped me from trying to be a card.

Now Jeannie was shouting. "Why not?"

"Because you know my idea of roughing it is when they don't leave the room service mint on the damn pillow!"

I heard another laugh quite clearly. All it did was reach out of the phone and make a quick little pull on my heart.

"When are you coming home, Mrs. Finley?"

The operator came on the line and said our time was up, then I heard Jeannie saying, "Talk to you in six days, I love you too, water those plants, Peter, I mean it."

Six days.

The dark continent was officially starting to wear my ass out.

CHAPTER

O'ROURKES had gone upscale.

Jimmy O'Rourke, my college roommate and East Side saloon legend, had purchased the apartment upstairs, gutted it, and then transformed it into an elegant dining area. O'Rourke referred to it as "the level of the duplex reserved for swells." It had light. It had space. It even had a piano. And hanging plants. It was a very nice room. The regulars just didn't think it was O'Rourkes, and wouldn't go upstairs.

"I can see why you boys don't like it," Jeannie said one night before she left for Africa. "It is kind of a radical change from the cave decor you all seem to fancy."

I said, "It's an atmosphere, not a decor. O'Rourkes is an idea, a state of mind."

"It's a dungeon," Jeannie said. "Wife hell."

"I need more tables," O'Rourke said.

I said, "I can't wait until the first night you stand at the top of the stairs and say, 'Oh boys, could you keep all that vulgar sports talk down, the people up here can't hear the piano.'"

O'Rourke turned to Jeannie and said, "He's always been resistant to change, you know."

"I know," she said. "I'm glad I wasn't around when bell-bottom jeans came in, it must have been ugly."

On this night, a lot of the regulars were scattered here and there around the room when I showed up at eight. Big Seamus was behind the bar, talking to a sharp lawyer from the baseball Players Association named Orza. Orza was one of our reigning trivia experts, and also a gourmet cook. He was explaining to Seamus that timing was everything when preparing *zabaglione*.

"It has to be made at the table," Orza said, "then served in heated glasses."

Seamus, looking bored, took care of a wet spot on the bar in front of Orza, then slipped a new napkin under his beer glass. Seamus said, "Everybody knows that."

Orza said, "If you let it go too long, it goes from the proper thickness to scrambled eggs."

Seamus said, "What you're saying is, you don't come in here for Jimmy's pecan pie, am I right?"

A group of the usual O'Rourkes suspects sat at the round corner table across from the bar, last stop before the back room. Kelly, the bearded desk guy from the *Daily News*, was there. So was a television producer named McGee, and Terry Cashman, the singer and songwriter who gave the world "Talkin' Baseball," the lovely ballad about Willie Mays and Mickey Mantle and Duke Snider. They had *The Baseball Encyclopedia* out as usual and were trying to figure out if anybody but Don Mattingly had gone over 230 hits and 20 home runs since Ducky Medwick.

The Baseball Encyclopedia was the only thing in O'Rourkes that had done more time there than Kelly and Cashman and McGee. And me.

Cashman said, "Look up Ted Williams." He was wearing a blue windbreaker that had *Baseball Video Magazine* in neat script across the front.

Kelly said, "He never had two-thirty, are you kidding? He walked too much."

McGee lit a long Benson and Hedges. "I think Frank is right." From upstairs, I could faintly hear Bob, the new man on the piano, fooling around with "All of Me." Then somebody started up the jukebox, and Bobby Darin started out about Mack the Knife, and it seemed to be business as usual at O'Rourkes, which never went off to Africa on a guy.

Jimmy O'Rourke and Marty were at a table all the way in the back. The Yankees were in Detroit. On the television above the back table, there was a blue tarp on the field at Tiger Stadium, then they cut to Bill White, on camera with Billy Martin, who looked like a dead person in a baseball uniform.

O'Rourke said, "Scribe, I hear you were at alma mater this afternoon." He was ready for summer. He had on a green blazer that looked like it had been lifted from Jack Nicklaus, and a purple Lacoste shirt. "Ask me where I was this afternoon."

Marty was sipping a Moosehead Ale and reading *The Wall Street Journal*. He said, "You're supposed to notice his tan before you ask, that's the point."

I looked more closely at O'Rourke. There was a certain bronze quality to his face. I was starting to think he looked more like Harpo Marx with black hair than Frank McHugh, the old character actor. His nose was peeling slightly.

"You didn't," I said. "It's too early."

O'Rourke beamed. "I am this color all over. First big afternoon of the year at Goody-land."

Goody-land was actually Camp Good Times, a nude beach O'Rourke had discovered down at the New Jersey shore. It was just another of the quirks that had made him endlessly entertaining to me since college.

He said, "I was once again at two with nature."

"At two?"

"Schoolteacher from Tenafly. She's coming by later."

From behind the newspaper Marty said, "I don't think you want to ask him what color her hair is."

I waved at Danny, the kid waiter, and he brought me a Jack Daniels. I had to watch it with the Jack before dinner. There was a crucial period early in the evening that dictated whether I would be home in bed for Letterman, or working over *The Baseball Encyclopedia* with Kelly and McGee and Cashman at four o'clock in the morning.

Danny said, "You got a call right before you walked in. Woman. Didn't want to leave a name."

"She say what she wanted?"

"Nope. But she sounded pissed off. I started to tell her you'd be in in a minute, on account of Marty told me, but she hung up."

I looked up at the television set, where they were taking the tarp off the field in Detroit.

"You think it was Lea?" Marty said.

"It must be. I haven't done anything that would make Natalie cranky enough to call from the coast. Jeannie I talked to before I came over here. Delores won't talk to me after office hours. The only ones who knew I was coming here were you and Lea. I'm just wondering what she wanted that couldn't wait until she got here, unless something came up and she couldn't come here."

Marty said, "Unless it wasn't her in the first place."

I chewed on a swizzle stick.

"We've been having this same conversation all day," I said.

Lea came in about fifteen minutes later. I saw her before she saw me. She was wearing the same clothes, but she wasn't the same coed. There was some juice to her now, some heat, I could see it all the way from the back room. Before I could get up I saw Seamus point in our direction. She walked briskly to where we sat, head high, eyes full of something.

It was one hell of an entrance, even for O'Rourkes.

She said, "Some sonofabitch rifled my room."

CHAPTER

I ASKED her if she wanted a drink.

"I don't drink," she said briskly, and ordered some hot tea instead. I watched her hands as she lit a cigarette. They were the most deliberate part of her. She was more angry than scared.

I waited until Danny brought her the tea before I asked her about it.

"Somebody picked the lock on my room, got in, and had a nice look around." She blew out some smoke. I got as much of it as I could. "Fucking bastard," she said.

"You sure it was picked?"

"Had to be. They're pretty strict about keys at The Square, especially with women. And it's supposed to be a killer dead-bolt. Somebody knew what he was doing."

Marty said, "Wouldn't someone have seen the some-one?"

"Not necessarily. You guys were at Julie's room this afternoon, right?"

We nodded.

Lea said, "Well, you could see what Weinstein is like. Maybe you remember, Peter. It's really just an old Village

57

apartment building. That's why it's always been such a hot dorm to live in. Because it's not really a dorm, even if you double up sometimes. I put my name on the waiting list after freshman year. Everybody wants to live in Weinstein because it has privacy but still's right on campus. The most rooms, or apartments, or whatever, on any floor is three.''

I'd noticed that on Julie Samson's floor. Two to your left as you came up the stairs, one to the right. Weinstein was private all right. But Marty and I had heard a lot of clumping on the stairs, and the music, when we were there. I told that to Lea.

"It was afternoon, between classes," she said. "It would be busy then. I'm guessing that whoever got into my room got in between seven and eight, in there. It would've been easy tonight. There's a big outdoor concert that started at six. Sort of an exam break. Group from The Square, actually, called Jimbo and the Bashers.''

O'Rourke said, "My favorites. Who'll ever forget their version of 'Begin the Beguine'?'' Lea smiled at O'Rourke. "Jimbo and the boys still wearing those Armani tuxedos?'' O'Rourke asked, and Lea smiled again.

College girls had always liked him. It was a gift.

"What was the breaker and enterer looking for, you think?'' Marty said.

"I have no idea,'' Lea said. "I really don't.''

I said, "We assuming this had something to do with Julie?''

She squeezed more lemon into her tea. "I wouldn't have if this hadn't been left taped to my bathroom mirror.'' She reached into her purse and pulled out a piece of lined white paper. "Leave it alone'' was typed on the paper.

I said, "Ah hah,'' and handed the paper to Marty. He handed it back to Lea and said, "You should have led the story with this.''

"Your typewriter?'' I said.

"Yes.''

"You call campus security?''

"No.''

"You call the cops?''

Shake of the head. "I'm sick of cops. I called you."

"And you don't have a roommate?"

"Uh uh."

I said, "Now, was the purpose of the visit to leave the note, or was the purpose of the visit to look for something and the note was an afterthought?"

Marty said, "Or a shot at scaring the first available redhead off the case?"

No one said anything. Marty watched the game. O'Rourke watched Lea, who shrugged and played with her lighter. I looked out at the front room where a roar of laughter came from the *Baseball Encyclopedia* table. Orza had joined the trivia players and gave a high five to Terry Cashman.

Marty said, "Maybe the one who broke in thought Lea found the money."

I looked at him. "Dr. Watson attack," I said. "That has to be it."

Lea said, "What money?"

I said to her, "You've been to Julie's room today, haven't you? You went over there after class to see if we were still there, right?"

"What money?"

Marty said to me, "That bag she carries would have been big enough, if someone happened to be watching the room, from either upstairs or downstairs, waiting to get in. Lea leaves, the guy goes in, checks the old Ferragamo vault, finds out the money's gone, remembers Lea's bag, goes and checks out Lea's room."

"Works for me."

Quietly Lea said, "What money, and right now, or I get pissed."

I told her about the ten thousand, and that we didn't think it had come from a money market fund. I took out the key and showed it to her. She said all the keys looked the same to her, like paper clips.

Lea said, "You think it's Michael Scalia?"

"I really don't have any idea," I said. "Whoever it is, I wonder why he or she waited to go after the stash. I am also wondering how someone knows enough about what you have been doing to want to stop you forthwith.''

As O'Rourke waved for Danny he said, "Forthwith?"

Marty smiled again. One in the afternoon, one at night. He was getting bubbly.

He said, "Somebody's bottom is chafing all of a sudden."

It was the news for the top of the hour.

"IT'S tough for me to feel like a grizzled veteran of TV news with you walking me home," Lea said.

We were at the front door of Weinstein. Across the street, Jimbo and the Bashers still had Washington Square Park rocking.

I said, "I'm the reason you got broken into. If I'd left the money where it was, persons unknown wouldn't have given you late maid service."

I jerked my head in the direction of the music. Or the music jerked my head in its direction.

"Do college persons still rock out?"

"Yes. They still rock out. When they don't jam out. Or rock on."

"You sure you're going to be all right?"

"I'm fine. Thanks for walking me." She leaned over and kissed me chastely on the cheek.

"You're not supposed to kiss your muscle," I said. "No one ever kisses their muscle."

"You still want to go see Sara Hildreth in the morning?"

"Meet me at my apartment. Eleven o'clock. Marty will pick us up there. We'll drive out to Douglaston and be there when she shows up for work at that place."

"Patrick's Pub."

"The very same. Also, while I'm thinking about it, sometime over the next couple of days, check out a history professor named Powell. Desmond Akeem Powell. He and Julie were friends."

"Desmond Akeem Powell?"

"I wouldn't make it up. He came by her room, and I'm sure he's a perfect gentleman. But he did come by the room."

"I'll check out the history professor." She walked through the door. I watched her into the elevator.

She had shown me which window was hers. I saw the light go on. Then I saw her wave. I walked across the park and leaned against Garibaldi, listening to some of the music. The driving drumbeat seemed to be everything; every so often Jimbo would jump across the stage and yell hoarsely into his microphone. After a while I got tired of Jimbo and started making my way uptown and east. Then I was standing at the bar at Pete's Tavern. It is at Eighteenth and Irving Place, down from Gramercy Park South. It is merely a New York landmark. The greatest saloon compliment you can pay Pete's is this: When old man Lavezzo decided there should be such a thing as P.J. Clarke's, he must have thought, Let's make it like Pete's.

The bar is in front, and across from the bar, up near the front door, is the booth where O. Henry is supposed to have written "Gift of the Magi." If it is a Pete's fiction, it is a fine fiction.

You eat in the back. The back is tables thrown close together and green-and-white checkered tablecloths and hustling waiters and good food, priced reasonably. Upstairs are a couple of party rooms. When the weather gets warm enough, you can sit out front. It is cozy, Pete's. And solid. You can talk or not talk. The television isn't on as much as in some of the uptown places like it, and the crowd isn't as collegiate as the joints closer to The Square. I ordered a Miller Lite. A young bartender brought it to me.

I thought about what I had.

I had a vulnerable girl, now dead, and a father who didn't come across as Andy Hardy's dad. I had a pushy roommate who'd left school. I had a slick boyfriend; he'd disappeared too. I had a transcript and ten thousand dollars and a three-thousand-dollar loan to the roommate. I had someone breaking into Lea Ballard's room. And leaving a note. Trying to scare.

Whoever it was didn't know it wouldn't work, mostly because scaring Marty and me is harder than listening to Dr. Ruth.

Someone wanted the money.

I thought, why?

And where did it come from?

Nobody had the answers at Pete's Tavern. I finished a second beer and took a cab home and watched the headline news on CNN and looked over Julie Samson's transcript and noticed something mildly interesting. I got into bed and listened to Larry King for about five minutes. He was interviewing some sportscaster doing a road company impression of Cosell.

I tried to read some of the Elmore Leonard western, but you don't mess around with Leonard, you give him your full attention.

I fell asleep during a commercial break on the King show. Another big day for the old grad.

CHAPTER
10

DOUGLASTON was part of Queens, but only on a geographic technicality. It would have survived fine as Gatsby territory. If you lived in Douglaston and had a view of Little Neck Bay, you had one of the postcard settings closest to Manhattan. And everyone tried to deal as bravely as they could with the fact that Bayside was the next stop west on the Long Island Railroad.

I knew a little bit about the town. In my newspaper days I had come out once to do a column about John McEnroe, who played his first tennis at the Douglaston Club. It was before McEnroe moved to Malibu, went to Lakers games with Jack Nicholson, married Ryan O'Neal's kid and stopped beating the key Eastern Europeans.

We took the Long Island Expressway out, got off at the Douglaston exit, took a right on Northern Boulevard and cruised east toward Little Neck, in what passes for Douglaston's downtown, until we saw Patrick's Pub on the right. It was noon on the button. It occurred to me again that for one reason or another I had spent more time in saloons than sawdust.

Marty parked the van. On the other side of the parking

area was an old-fashioned barber shop with the pole spinning in front. Down the street a couple of blocks on the other side was a Howard Johnson's restaurant, the orange and blue looking funny as always. I remembered vaguely that there was some great hamburger joint named Scooby or Scobee nearby, but wasn't sure whether it was in Little Neck or Douglaston. Directions were getting a little rougher for me as I got older. It was from living with J.B. Finley, who'd spent her New York lifetime getting out of cabs and restaurants, starting to walk down the street, stopping, saying, "Which way is Third?"

Marty came around with the sound equipment and handed it to Lea. He said, "Congratulations, kid, you're in show business."

Lea watched him walk back to get the Betacam and the rest of the stuff.

"He's great," she said. "But then you know that, right?"

"I just can't decide whether he should be Hope or Crosby when we start making the *Road* movies," I said.

Lea said, "You still think it's better just to pop in on Sara instead of setting something up?"

"I'm sure she knows something is up because I called and asked what time she was working today. And something tells me she knows we've been nosing around The Square. She probably knows that questions are being asked, anyway. Why give the girl time to prepare her lines? That's my position and I'm sticking to it."

We were at the door to Patrick's Pub. Marty said, "Or she could tell you to honk off."

I said, "There is that consideration, I won't lie to you."

There is always something faintly derelict, seamy, about walking into a bar in the daytime; it's a skipping-school feeling for drinkers. But Patrick's Pub was actually nicer than I expected. It fit the proper darkness requirements. There was a lot of wood, and no pictures of leprechauns that I could see. It was bigger than I expected, with plenty of restaurant room, and enough space for the ones at the bar to go three or four deep.

The bartender, who ran to Marty's size, was putting together some bloody Mary mixer. There was an old man at one end of the bar. He wore a pinstriped suit. There was a shot of something amber in front of him. A waiter in a white dress shirt and black slacks and white Reebok tennis shoes was taking chairs off a table.

There was a small dark woman at the end of the bar where the bartender was now shaking up the bloody Mary fixings.

I said, "Her?"

Lea said, "Her."

Sara Hildreth did not notice us until Marty set the lights down and the clatter of that reverberated around Patrick's Pub, empty except for our three and their three and the seersucker man with the shot.

It got unusual then.

Sara Hildreth turned around and skipped through the swing doors leading into the kitchen. I took it as more than on-camera shyness and followed her. As I got to the doors the bartender looked up with mild surprise, or maybe great surprise for him, and said, "Hey, you can't go in there, buddy." He started to step out in front of me. Marty stepped in front of him like a basketball pick and said, "What do you have in diet soft drinks?" I got into the kitchen just in time to see Sara Hildreth, quick little bug, go out the back door.

She was about thirty yards ahead of me, moving past Marty's van toward Northern Boulevard when I got outside. She had a nice organized stride with tight little arm movements, head high, back arched, Reeboks eating up the ground. I thought, Wonderful, I'm chasing Joan Benoit.

She took a left at Suzanne's Fur Shop. I wondered briefly if I would have such a great eye for detail if I could still run. She was a solid thirty ahead of me and I wasn't making a dent in the lead. It was turning into a silly-looking chase. I was already sweating. We passed Magic Realty and Marketo Antiques and a place called the Sports Connection; a big blond guy in the window of the Sports Connection gave me a thumbs up sign and mouthed, Go for it. I gave him the finger. I was hoping somewhere not too far west on Northern Boulevard there was a crossing street and a light and some traffic so Sara Hildreth and I could stop all this bracing physical exercise.

I was also hoping there weren't any Heartbreak Hills on this particular course.

We passed the Actyve Travel Agency. It was on a corner. There was a steady stream of traffic coming from the left, which meant we were close to the LIE. Most of the cars were making right turns. She had to stop. She let one car pass then started to cross Northern, but the horn of the next car stopped her. When she turned her head to see where I was, I was right there, corner of Northern and Brownvale. It had been a hard couple of hundred yards. My breath sounded like the whistling of a teapot. She started to take off again, but I grabbed hold of her arm.

"Tag, pumpkin," I said. "You're it."

"I'M Peter Finley," I said.

Icebreaker.

We were walking back toward Patrick's Pub, makers of a wary, silent truce. I had let go of her arm when she agreed not to run away. She was behind me now, a sullen presence. I didn't know about the Hildreth side of the family, but somebody on the other side had come from Italy once. Her hair was black as her mood.

She said, "I know who you are. And I don't want to talk to you."

"It happens," I said. "But not everybody makes a break for it."

She looked at me. There was nothing to read in her face. She really was quite pretty. Too petite for my taste, but a neat package. She said, "Is this where we start to establish some rapport? Forget it, pal."

"Pal?" I said. "You call cops dirty screws?"

"Right," she said. She looked at me again. "Are you going to leave when we get to Patrick's or am I going to leave? It would be better if it was you, because I need this job."

We were standing in front of the Sports Connection. The blond guy eyeballed me. He was bigger than I'd noticed on the run. Even his hair looked like it lifted weights.

I said, "Listen, I have no idea why my presence out here has you spooked the way it does. You know I'm here to ask about Julie Samson. She was your roommate, and she was supposed to be your friend. I'm trying to find out why she did what she did. You don't want to help me. Maybe I should loan you three grand like she did. That help, pal?"

I thought for a moment she was getting her little self organized to take a slap. She didn't, and all the spit went out of her eyes fast as it got in there.

"Fuck you."

"See, now we've got a nice, healthy dialogue going."

"Who told you about the money?"

"Arthur Samson."

We were walking again.

She said, "The great Arthur Samson. You probably never met anybody as warm as him, right?"

I went with her. "He's never going to pass for the head of the local Lion's Club."

"He's a bullying, abusive drunk," she said. "There were times when I wondered if he could have picked Julie out of a goddamn lineup. Dear old dad. He is some sonofabitch. He was the reason she was so scared of the world. She was in training her whole life, being scared of *him*."

"What do you mean, scared of him?"

"Are you kidding?" she said. Then she stopped herself, shook her head. "Forget it. Won't work. I'm not supposed to talk to you about anything. He said . . ."

I had a feeling the wrong things had fallen out of Sara Hildreth's mouth.

"Who said?"

She sighed. "Leave it alone. Please? You wanted me to tell you something? Here it is. Don't get into this. It isn't worth it. I really haven't said anything to you, okay? But I've said more than I should have. Just leave it alone. Let her rest in peace. She deserves that much. If anybody should ask you, I called in sick today, you couldn't find me."

I said, "Damn, you're a great friend. People must come to Douglaston from all over Long Island, just to see a friend like you."

We were back in front of Patrick's Pub. She started to walk in the door. I grabbed her by the arm.

"What are you so afraid of? *Who* are you so afraid of? What the hell made you so afraid that you left school the way you did?"

She gave me a hard look. I thought she might be having a conversation with herself.

I said, "I can help you. This is what I do. I'm good at this."

All the fight was out of her. She made no move to get free of me. But she didn't say anything.

"You don't want to tell me anything? Deal. You don't know me. But I've got Lea Ballard with me. You know her. Talk to her. Arthur Samson gave me a little. You've given me a little just because someone has you as spooked as you are. But I've got to know what Julie was into. I've got to know what was going on. I've got to find Michael Scalia. You know where he is?"

In a small voice, small enough to hold in your hand, she said, "Leave it alone. It won't be you that'll get hurt. Do you understand?"

I opened the door to Patrick's Pub, and let her walk in ahead of me. There were a few more people at the bar. The waiter was handing menus to a couple of teenagers seated at one of the tables. The bartender had turned on the television set, which was showing some video with a lot of smoke and green-haired women on MTV.

"Just tell me where to find Scalia," I said. "Or where to look. Lea says nobody's seen him. He didn't go to the funeral. He hasn't been seen at his apartment, according to the doormen anyway, Lea checked. Is it him you're afraid of?"

She stopped. In a voice smaller than the one outside, she said, "In a minute, I'm going to yell at you to leave me alone, and I'm going to walk away from you. Shit, I must be crazy. But maybe you should think about having dinner some night at Knickerbocker's. You know it? On University?"

I told her I did.

She said, "Okay, then."

Then she yelled at me to leave her the hell alone, and

everybody in Patrick's Pub turned to stare at me as she stormed past Marty and Lea at the end of the bar and back into the kitchen.

I yelled "Bitch!" after her, threw up my arms in disgust, walked back through the door and into the parking lot.

When we were all in the van for the ride back to the city, Marty Pearl mentioned he thought I might have been chewing on the furniture a bit too much there at the end with the bitch stuff, and the big exit.

I said to him, "You don't understand motivation or the Method or any of that shit, do you?"

Marty adjusted the rearview mirror slightly.

"That stuff I understand," he said. "Here's what I don't understand: When you had to pick an acting school, why the Nutty Professor's?"

 TOLD Lea I would come fetch her about eight o'clock and we would see what we could see at the Knickerbocker Bar and Grill. I told her I would have gone to Knickerbocker's alone, but she knew what Scalia looked like. Marty said for both of us to have a ball, he had a date.

I said, "Car date? Or meet her in front of the movies?"

"Car date."

"With who?"

Marty grinned, or just wanted to exercise the ends of his mouth. "I can't send you behind enemy lines with that sort of information."

"Okay, okay," I said. "With *whom*? But that's as far as I go, mister."

He shook his head.

"I hate when you do this," I said.

We were back at The Square, Marty dropping Lea and me off in front of the arch. She said she had an appointment she didn't want to miss. I was going to see Gus Dancy, an old professor of mine; I'd noticed in Julie's transcript she'd been taking one of his seminars. It was called "Contemporary Thought." It sounded like Gus, only with him you could take out contemporary and put in radical. I didn't know how much he could give me for the story, but he had been the number one faculty star at Washington Square University back in the late sixties and early seventies, and a hero to P. Finley and a lot of other people when the waiting list to get in to one of his classes was like one for an exclusive country club. I hadn't seen him in years, and I was glad I had a reason.

"You're really not going to tell me who she is?" I said to Marty.

He said, "There's no reason why both of us should be in danger. I'll give you information on a need-to-know basis."

Lea was looking at us like we were Lucy and Ethel.

"She work at the station? You could at least tell me if she works at the station."

He shook his head again. "Talk to you later," he said, and got back in the van, honked the horn twice, and made the left toward University.

"I could follow the sonofabitch," I said.

Lea laughed. "How long did you say your wife has been in Africa?" She reached into her purse for what looked like a train schedule, only thicker, found what she wanted in it, tossed it back in her purse. "Anything I can do this afternoon? No classes later, boss."

"As a matter of fact, there is. I know you told me Julie liked to keep to herself. But she had to have other friends other than the enigmatic Miss Hildreth. Talk to them. Check 'em out. If you think I should talk to some of them too, okay on that. Some of them must live in Weinstein. Maybe she was always having a pajama party with someone, or borrowing stockings, or dope."

Lea said, "She wasn't a doper."

"You're sure about that?"

"I didn't know her all that well, but I knew her well enough to know that. There are signs. You hear things. You can tell."

"Really."

She said calmly, "Really."

I thought, she's like no coed I ever knew. Not even Jeannie. Those eyes had seen things. I didn't know what. Things.

"Whatever," I said. "I want to know how the hell she spent her time. Maybe she did have a job nobody knew about."

Lea said, "Check. I'll check." And headed uptown on Fifth, opposite direction of school.

I said, "Hey, you're going the wrong way."

She turned around, walked backward for a few steps. "Club meeting," she yelled.

"What club? Four-H? Chess Club? Young Americans for Freedom?"

She yelled, "Talk to you later."

First, Sara Hildreth. Now Marty and Lea. Everybody wanted to talk to me later.

Everybody had secrets except the talent.

YOU had to be there. You had to see Gus Dancy standing at a podium at The Square in those days, voice full of rage, stopping every once in a while to put down the papers in his hands and raise a clenched fist to me and all the students filling the park, then picking up the papers and again reading the names of the dead from Vietnam. There were a lot of teachers who didn't walk into the park for those sorts of demonstrations in those angry days. Gus Dancy did. Gus Dancy organized them.

He wasn't only our star. He was the faculty star of the city, leading marches, appearing on television shows, debating Bill Buckley, writing cover stories for *The Sunday New York Times* Magazine defending the radical left. We all thought he was fucking Churchill.

He had long blond hair and a preacher's voice and wore jeans and work shirts and corduroy jackets, and to us he always looked like he'd walked off the cover of *Esquire*. If you couldn't get into his classes, you could find him sometimes at our drinking joints, Chumley's or Gil's or Googie's, drinking Wild Turkey at one of the tables, nobody talking much except him. When they tried to close down the school paper—ironically and unfortunately known even in those days as *The Square Deal*—Gus Dancy wrote a front-page editorial that was good as his resignation if anybody from the administration tried to remove so much as a comma from our offices.

When I got to his office on the third floor of the Kornheiser Library building, Dancy wasn't there. He wasn't supposed to have a three o'clock class, I'd checked, but there was no answer when I knocked on the door, and no sounds from behind it. I hadn't called because I wanted to surprise him. The last time I'd talked to him had been for a newspaper column the day after John Lennon died. I wanted to write about an eighties event that really signaled the end of the sixties once and for all. I came down to The Square and met Gus and we sat out in the park where he'd made some of his speeches, and he filled my notebook.

He said that day, "That reunion concert the Beatles never had was going to be the last great event of the sixties, wasn't it? I was very much hoping they would have it at Shea Stadium. I thought that would be a very nice way of tying things up. But now Lennon is dead and there will be no reunion concert, and perhaps it is time for us all to let go."

I handed him my notebook when he was finished and grinned. "Good luck with the column. Make it about eight hundred words and try to get it done by six o'clock, or the desk guys will start to snarl like pit bulls."

Now I couldn't decide whether to go or wait, but I was there so I waited outside his door the way I had a lot of times in college, when the paper was in trouble, or I thought I was. Gus would come back finally and shake an unfiltered Camel out of a battered pack and we would talk it out.

I wondered if he still smoked Camels. I wondered if he ever got married, since he had been a legendary rake back when O'Rourke and I were at The Square. Gus's teaching and oratory never impressed O'Rourke much, but his rumored prowess with women made O'Rourke want to save his baseball card.

I wondered if his wife, if he had one, thought she was the Surgeon General of the United States. I assumed that somewhere in Africa, Jeannie was saying to the white hunter, "He's looking to bum a cigarette right now, I feel it. He has the discipline of a two-year-old."

Then I heard a familiar voice saying, "If they lay their stinking hands on one Olivetti, we'll slap an injunction on their soft white asses, right?"

I looked up and figured everything at The Square had changed except Gus Dancy.

"Shit, Gus," I said, shaking his hand, "you don't look anything like Mr. Chips."

He unlocked the door, gave me a big hearty slap on the back as he led me in.

"It's all illusion," he said, and tossed a battered old leather briefcase on a battered couch of dying print. "If I'm not any older, neither are you."

"The notion is practically geometrical in its precision."

His office was on the side facing Wirth.

I said, "I thought after all these years you'd at least have a view of the park, Gus. I thought a park view was faculty heaven."

"You never used to complain about the pawnshop decor," he said.

The room had gotten more cluttered in my years away from The Square. But it was the same look: Part pawnshop, part secondhand bookstore, part wardrobe dumping ground. Except for all the books, it was the messy teenager's room in a sitcom. There were bookshelves built around the door and over the door and into all the walls, but you could barely see the shelves in the side walls for the stacks of books in front of them, stacks as tall as I was. I figured if you could crack Gus Dancy's filing systems you could have cracked all the Nazi codes in World War II. On top of the stacks were corduroy sports jackets, and blue jeans, an old Burberry raincoat, a pea coat, scarves. A pair of old sheepskin gloves. He took off the sports jacket he was wearing, tossed it over the back of his chair, motioned me into the chair across the desk from him. To his right, there was a small refrigerator, almost completely hidden by books, except for the off-white door that features an old sticker from the Village Gate. He opened it, took out a Budweiser, offered the can in my direction.

"Little early," I said. I waved a hand at the room. "Gus, you could still hide political prisoners in here."

He shrugged, settled into his own chair, put weathered motorcycle boots up on his desk. He toasted me wordlessly. Then he drank beer.

"Or hide a career, perhaps," he said. "But I still like it up here. It was always the contradiction with me, right? I wanted to change everything in the world except the world around me. Around me, I wanted everything to stay the same. Alas, alas. Give me power to the people, and some Gershwin tunes."

He drank more beer. I thought he looked tired. And thinner than I remembered. He wasn't a body builder to begin with. And, at closer inspection, there was a lot of gray in his hair now. I was surprised to find myself thinking the shoulder length of it looked silly. Like a bad hairpiece.

I said, "Didn't I read something in one of those silly alumni bulletins about your being made head of your department?"

"Ah, yes. The tenured boot upstairs. A change of administration, a big jump to the right of center like most of America as we changed decades, and, of course, a bit of discomfort concerning the radical teachings and rebellious presence of Augustus Dancy. To the tight-assed little men now running your alma mater, old Finley, I was as welcome a reminder of the past as a splash of paint on the side of a building, or a busted window. What do we do with Dancy? I was not their kind. So they raised my salary because they couldn't fire me and gave me a title and let me keep two classes. And this office. Old Finley, you are actually sitting in the Dancy Museum."

He set the empty beer can down on the desk, and gave his head and hair a big shake, like a wet dog.

"I'm sorry. It has not been a good day. There was a difficulty with the first and second races at Belmont."

I laughed, trying to cut through a gloom I didn't really want to know about. Dancy was marking up memories of Dancy and I didn't like it. I felt like I was watching one of those Bing Crosby television specials, when he was old.

Crosby looked thin and frail, but when it came time to sing "White Christmas," he just lip-synced the sucker, so the voice was the same if nothing else was.

"Gus, you still play the ponies?"

He reached into the middle drawer of his desk and pulled out a *Daily Racing Form* that looked like it had been corrected in red ink. Like one of his test papers.

"It is," he said, voice suddenly filled with the old brio, "a course I shall pass before I die." He stuffed the paper back into his desk and said, "So, to what do I owe the honor of this visit from the noted investigator of Channel . . ."

"A," I said.

"Of course. Down the alphabet from the smutty public access channels."

Behind him, between two windows, was a photograph of Gus Dancy, arm casually thrown around the shoulder of Jane Fonda. It was pre-aerobics. Jane still had hips.

I said in a serious tone that I think surprised him, "I'm looking for information about a former student of yours, Julie Samson. I'm down here checking into her suicide, and when I was going over her transcript, I noticed that she took one of your courses. Contemporary Thought?"

He grinned. "Contemporary Thought is not one of my courses, old Finley. It is *the* course. It is *the* course and *the* department I now run. The department is Contemporary Thought, and so are the two classes of it I teach, one for freshmen, the other for upperclassmen. You could say I *am* contemporary thinking on this campus, maybe on the East Coast. Two seminars. Twelve students in each. They are what tenure and twenty years of passion have earned me at this institution."

It was not talk of him I wanted. It was talk of her. For the first time, I found myself annoyed at Gus Dancy. It was just what I needed to make myself feel even older than I was already feeling.

"Julie Samson, Gus. She took the course this semester."

"Yes. Until all that beauty went to waste and no form of contemporary thinking could help her. Nothing quite like it has ever happened around here, at least not in my experience. We've had deaths before, and some suicides. But nothing quite so, how would you describe it, garishly tragic.'' He got up and helped himself to another beer. "But why does she interest you? Aren't you always after the ones with the black hats, the serious baddies? You chase them and catch them.''

"I hear you, Gus. But there are some unusual circumstances around this girl's death. So here I am. It's alma mater. It's a serious bad thing. I think there's a story here.''

I told him about the mugging, or whatever it was, and Lea's suspicions and Sara Hildreth and Michael Scalia and Lea's room being broken into. I did not tell him about the ten thousand dollars that lived in a shoe box.

When I finished he said, "Obviously you think there is a connection to all of it.''

"Yeah, I do. I don't know how. But I want to know more about Julie Samson.''

"There was beauty there,'' he said softly. He had always been able to play his voice the way Benny Goodman played the stick, bringing it up, taking it down, doing up-tempo and ballads. "I don't just mean physical beauty. There was this quiet part of her bathed in light. But she would not show it, at least not often enough. It was as if she were afraid of her own quality somehow.''

"Enough to kill herself?''

He mashed the beer can like a jock at a fraternity party, or one of those bruisers in the commercials. "Such a waste! I think anyone who knew her wondered afterward if something could have been done, if some reaching out would have made a difference. It is the most cruel kind of second-guessing, isn't it?''

I said, "She had a gun. She had to get the gun somewhere, but she doesn't seem to be the type who would even know how to get a damn handgun, much less use it. Where does she get the gun?''

"A friend perhaps. The young man, Scalia?''

"You know him?''

He took his time, aimed the mashed beer can at the wastebasket across the room, one-handed it like a basketball free throw. Missed. "Michael Scalia? He was in my seminar too. A bit of a hood, that one, but the shame is, he does have a crackerjack mind, a rather unique way of looking at the world. But college seemed to be a hobby with him, like he was trying to see whether anything from the straight world appealed to him. They don't burn for knowledge the way they did in your day, old Finley. Ideas are no longer weapons. They all look for angles."

I was starting to think he might be drunk. In and out. Out and in. Like a car trying to hold the road. He wasn't really focusing on me, or the conversation. I thought, Christ, he looks old after all.

"She a good student, Gus?"

He stared at me: like a student jolted out of a reverie. "Yes. And pleasantly creative, in that quiet way. One of her assignments earlier in the semester was about how to run a radical business. Something from the old days, eh? I was just looking for some progressive thought, a way for them to think of money-making in terms of something that might be mildly useful to society, if you will. She did well with it. She called for a total woman counseling service for sex discrimination cases, from legal counseling to psychotherapy. She seemed to have quite a good grasp of the therapy end of it. Startlingly good, as a matter of fact. The subject of battered women, women battered in any way, seemed to strike a chord in her. The paper worked on several levels. It was exciting for me to see someone else excited about the concept of being progressive in the marketplace. It doesn't happen that way so often. It made me feel like I still had my heater."

"Was it obvious to you that she and Scalia were an item?"

"No, actually. I did not make that connection until you told me. Bit of a mismatched pair, those two, wouldn't you say? Beauty and the beast."

I said, "Beast?"

He grinned. "Actually more of a shark, old Finley. Quick and smart, but a predator down deep."

"You think he could be in it somewhere?"

"In what? The middle of a muddle? What are you looking for, after all? Is there a chance the girl might rest more gently if left alone?'' He fooled with a bowl of paper clips at the corner of the desk. ''But that was never your nature, was it? Not even on the college paper. You were always a shark too, when there were answers floating about.''

I made a show of looking at my watch, like, oh shit, where has the time gone?

I said, ''Maybe there's nothing out there, you know, Gus. But I gotta know.'' I stood up. ''You want to have dinner? Tomorrow night, maybe?''

''A splendid idea. It will keep me away from the track. I find myself sampling the cuisine of the Meadowlands restaurants far too often. Two and three times a week sometimes. It is not conducive to healthy digestion, or a healthy bank account, old Finley. You and I will dine tomorrow evening, and I will try not to bore you with rancor, as I did today. And perhaps I will remember something useful about the fair Julie.''

I said, ''Tomorrow night, then, okay? We'll have a few drinks and talk about what young lions we used to be, and I'll embarrass you and tell you how much you always meant to me.''

Gus Dancy went back into the middle drawer of his desk for the *Racing Form*, turned some pages in it. ''Having said all that, I will now direct my attention to tonight's racing at the Meadowlands. Home away from home. Where the afternoon losers look for solace.''

I left him there with the ponies.

In the hall, I said out loud, ''Shit.''

My return to alma mater was turning out to be a regular Rudy Vallee musical. Maybe O'Rourke could play Jack Oakie, we could all wear varsity sweaters and sing the school song.

CHAPTER

12

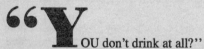

OU don't drink at all?"

Lea said, "Nope."

We were at the Knickerbocker Bar and Grill at University and Ninth, sitting at one of the round tables in the front part of the room, near the bar. It was eight-thirty. The place was beginning to fill up. Junior Nance was already at the piano. Junior Nance has black skin and white hair, and when he smiles I think he looks like what Magic Johnson will look like when he's as old as Junior. He is an elf who plays jazz piano that is full of fun. Junior has all the moves. The Lord gave him touch, too.

He was tickling "Dark Town Strutter's Ball," an Ellington thing. You didn't come to Knickerbocker's to watch baseball with the sound off. You came for Junior. He was sport enough.

Or you came for Michael Scalia, if your tastes were more eclectic.

I said to Lea, "You won't have a beer?"

She shook her head.

"Glass of wine?"

"Nope."

"Okay," I said. "You're at a New Year's Eve party. It's one minute to midnight. Everybody raises their glass of champagne and gets ready to sing 'Auld Lang Syne.' You don't raise your glass?"

"Of course I raise my glass, silly."

"But there's no champagne in it."

She blew some cigarette smoke at the ceiling, where it joined the rest of the smoke in Knickerbocker's. I wanted to go up there after it. "Apple juice," she said. "Or ginger ale. Or club soda."

She was facing the front door. I was sitting to her right. I could look out the front window and across the street. Lea would be able to spot Scalia if he walked in. I would be right there if there was trouble at the Aphrodite Cleaners or the Lafayette Cleaners on the other side of University, or the Meurice Cleaners next door. The sign in front of Meurice said, "Send your fur to Camp Meurice."

In Manhattan, you can never find a taxicab in the rain or a policeman when you really need one. But there isn't a block in the entire borough where you can't get a shirt cleaned and pressed in a jiffy.

I was nursing an Amstel. Lea had a club soda with lime in front of her. We were passing the time, hoping Michael Scalia would show, listening to Junior. The conversation started when I jokingly asked why she never ordered a real drink, was she a closet Christian Scientist?

I said, "So you're basically telling me you're on the wagon."

She said, "I'm retired." She pursed her lips and frowned. "You look like this," she said. "You're not getting it, are you?"

"I just thought everybody in college drank. It wasn't ever a scientific study. Like it wasn't from the *New England Journal of Medicine*. But I drank. O'Rourke drank. All our friends drank. We all assumed it was part of the curriculum."

She nodded.

"I'm an alcoholic," Lea said. It came out smoothly, like she'd said, "I have great legs," or "I have red hair." She sipped some club soda, giving a look at the door. "Those club meetings I go to are Alcoholics Anonymous meetings."

Junior Nance was taking the A train now.

"You're kidding," I said. "AA? Come on. You're too—"

"Young to be a rummy? Good-looking? How about too nice? I'm allergic to alcohol. Any kind. I'm twenty-three years old. Most seniors are twenty-two. I took a year off, went back to Boston and worked in an Ann Taylor, and started going to AA. Full time, not dabbling. On the eighth of June at approximately six o'clock in the morning, I'll have been sober for two years." She took the glass of club soda again and clicked it against my beer bottle, which was in my hand. "Cheers," she said.

I looked at her. She had a navy polo shirt tucked into white jeans. She didn't wear jewelry, no chains, no earrings. She was the best-looking woman in the place. I supposed I didn't know what AA looked like, but I didn't think it looked like her.

I said, "How come you're telling me this?" I saw her eyes dart toward the door. I turned around slowly. It was a dark-haired kid, about six feet, walking in with a tiny blonde who reminded me of Jane Powell in *Royal Wedding*. Lea shook her head no.

"I'm telling you because now we've been in two bars, and both times when I didn't order a real drink, you looked at me like I'd taken my shirt off. I'm not embarrassed about talking about it if you're not embarrassed hearing it. I just couldn't drink. A hell of a lot of my friends can't drink, but they haven't stopped. If I didn't stop, I was going to end up dead. I really believe that. When I'd have two drinks, I was off. I wanted ten. Then I wanted some dope if anybody had any. Then there were times when I woke up in places with guys I shouldn't have. And know what? Even with all that, I thought what I was doing was normal. Then I read this book for a psych class. It was called *The Courage to Change* by this guy named Wholey. It's got all these first-person testimonies by these famous recovering alcoholics. All of a sudden, my own life was like jumping off the pages at me. Did my personality change when I drank? You bet it did. Was I thinking about the next one before I finished the one I had in front of me? Double your bet. On and on. The book said call AA. I called. I got a schedule. I found out there were meetings all over the city, just about every hour of the day. So I finally screwed up some courage and went to a beginner's meeting. And just like that, before I knew what I was saying, I put my hand up and said, 'My name is Lea, I'm an alcoholic.' That was that. I drank on and off for a couple more months, then I stopped. It was then I took the year off. You wouldn't have liked me back then. I'm a lot nicer now."

She stopped and lit another cigarette. Across the street, in front of Lafayette Cleaners, a skinny kid in cut-off jeans and high-top sneakers stopped, did a back flip, landed like a Rumanian gymnast, and kept walking.

I said to Lea, "Your parents know?"

"My father doesn't like the idea at all, because he's an active alcoholic too, even if he denies it. I love him, but if he doesn't stop he's going to be dead before he's sixty."

I didn't know what to say about that. Since I had always fancied myself the touring pro from O'Rourkes, I didn't know what to say about any of it. But once again I figured that if you could just retain all the things you learn in saloons, you could put the public library right out of business.

Then Lea said, "Turn around slowly, no big deal," just as the dinner crowd in the back part of the room began to applaud Junior Nance. I turned slowly. He was black-haired, shorter than I expected, with a silk sports jacket and pressed blue jeans and a black T-shirt underneath the sports jacket.

Lea said, "Him."

I said, "Michael Scalia, you cute thing."

Then I told Lea to scram.

"WHAT?" she said.

"Amscray."

"How come?"

"Doesn't matter how come. Beat it. *Adios muchachos.* Go with God." I moved my chair a little and saw Scalia sit down at a table near the piano. "No fooling. When the waitress comes over to take his drink order, get up, keep your gorgeous mug facing the door, and get out of here.''

She said, "I'm staying."

"You're going, kiddo. He probably knows what you look like. If he does happen to be the one who got into your room, he definitely must know what you look like. But I'd rather he didn't see us together. I don't know if I'm going to talk to him or follow him or what, but I don't want you around."

"He could know what you look like. You're on television. And if he was watching Weinstein the other day, he saw you go to Julie's room and he saw you come out."

I reached down to the floor and grabbed her bag and stuck it in her lap.

"Are you enjoying your new career in the challenging world of television reporting?"

"Uncle," Lea said. The waitress, we saw, was between Scalia and us. Lea got up, cut through a new crowd of laughers and shouters coming into Knickerbocker's, took a right on Tenth when she hit the street, and kept going. I left some money on the table and went and stood at the corner of the bar, which was starting to get busy.

I ordered another beer and the bartender put it in front of me. I didn't know how I wanted to play it with Scalia. I didn't have a thing on him. He was the boyfriend. He had the ability to scare the eye shadow off Sara Hildreth, who otherwise seemed a hard case. Gus Dancy had called him a shark, and that probably went double for Arthur Samson. I had no proof he'd tapped Lea's room. I didn't know how he was related to the ten thousand, if he was at all.

I sipped my beer and finally thought, Come out of your shell, Finley.

Meet people.

Junior Nance sat back down after a short break. He started sneaking up on "Satin Doll." It was apparently going to be Ellington all the way.

I walked over to Scalia's table, sat down across from him and said, "How you doing, Mike?"

It didn't ruffle him much. He looked bored. He took a drink of something amber on the rocks. His jacket came up his arm a little and I noticed his watch was a Cartier if it wasn't a knock-off.

He said, "I know you?" And looked at the door.

"You're expecting someone, aren't you?" I said amiably. "Hell, if this is a bad time, you just say the word."

Scalia leaned forward. He had what Jeannie called gigolo good looks. Hair was a little too slick, tan a little too serious. He smelled, I thought, like lilacs.

"You smell like a million bucks," I said.

"Listen," he said. "I don't want any trouble. The man is playing the piano. I've got a pretty girl coming to meet me. I don't know who you are, or what you want. Don't start something you don't know how it will end."

"My name is Peter Finley," I said. "But I think you know that already. Whether you do or not is actually sort of irrelevant. I'm looking into the death of Julie Samson. People tell me you and Julie were dating or whatever. I want to talk to you about her, if you can find a way to keep your grief from spilling all over the place."

He looked at the door again, then at Junior, then at me.

"What if I don't want to talk to you?" he said. "What if I get up from the table and walk away and leave you sitting here being a snappy comic all by yourself?"

"That is a fair question, junior. You don't mind if I call you junior? Okay, then. You get up, I'll follow you. I'm sure you're probably a tough guy on campus, but I'll get you outside and pull your pants down and your jacket over your head."

We looked at each other. I said, "Here's what I'm thinking, junior: I'm thinking your girlfriend killed herself not long ago, and you seem to be bearing up awfully fucking well. Would you call that a reasonable assessment of where we are?"

He didn't say anything right away. I got this picture of him rolling dice inside his slick moussed-up semi-crewcut black hair, deciding how to play it. He smiled finally.

"Listen," he said. "I don't want us to have an attitude here. You startled me a bit, sitting down out of the blue that way. I got a little pissed. Now I'm not pissed." He held out a hand. "Michael Scalia."

I shook it, smiling back at him. I was smiling because I was thinking he must have learned his charm from old Rat Pack movies.

He had a thin gold bracelet on the same wrist as his watch.

"How can I help you? Really."

"You were dating Julie before she died. I thought you might know what was bothering her."

"Let me get one thing straight with you, Mr. Finley." He looked down and flicked something off the arm of his jacket. "I did date Julie for a while last fall. Then we broke up. She came back, asked that we give it another try around Christmas. Then we broke up again. She called me for a while, but I finally convinced her it was over. I haven't seen her . . . I didn't see her much in the months before she shot herself."

"Was there anything unusual going on in her life while the two of you were dating?"

"No. I mean, not that I noticed, and we spent a lot of time together. She was introverted, you know. She didn't have much confidence in herself. But being with me seemed to loosen her up. Like, I think it was good that we came from different worlds. Her from daddy's big house in the suburbs, and me from East Tenth. I don't think she ever enjoyed the city so much until we started going out."

"You slept together?"

"Sure."

"How come you broke up? You have a fight? She meet somebody else? You drop her?"

He laughed and showed off ridiculously even teeth.

"All of the above," he said. "We had a fight. It was me who met someone else. Dropped sounds like kid stuff. You know, in light of what happened to her. We stopped seeing each other, and it was my idea."

I said, "You got any theories about the gun?"

Scalia was looking at the door, and the dinner crowd was applauding again.

"What?"

"Where would she get a gun? Girl from the suburbs. Quiet, introverted, et cetera, et cetera. It's not easy to get a gun. I mean, it's easy for a Goetz, but you'd think it would be a bitch for Julie Samson, wouldn't you?"

Scalia said, "When I, you know, found out, I thought the same thing, as a matter of fact."

"It wouldn't have been your gun, would it?"

"No. But why would you think it was?"

"I don't know. You look like a tough guy, junior."

He said, "Hey." Took a drink. "I thought we were getting along here. Maybe you could lose junior now."

He had a signet ring on his right pinky, not too big, not too small. I said, "How come you didn't show up for the funeral?"

"How do you know I didn't?"

"I know things. I'm a Pisces."

"Her father hated my guts, okay? We hadn't seen each other for months, you know, socially. I didn't want to cause any kind of scene. I didn't think I belonged there."

The waitress came over. I put my hand over my beer glass. Scalia winked at her and shook his head no. The waitress smiled back at him.

I said, "How well do you know Sara Hildreth?"

It was like he counted out the old pass-rush count from touch football. One Mississippi, two Mississippi.

"Pretty well," he said, after two Mississippi. "She was Julie's roommate. The three of us did things together."

"You heard from her much lately?"

Three Mississippi.

"We spoke on the phone, you know, after."

"You haven't seen her?"

"This is important?"

"Humor me."

"No, I haven't seen her. She left school, right? Went home? I think she's working in Douglaston someplace, she told me, in some bar."

Scalia looked at his watch.

"Listen, I really am meeting someone soon, late as she is. You want to do this again, fine." He reached into his pocket, took out a notebook, ripped out a piece of paper, put the notebook back in his jacket. I wanted to know how come it didn't mess up the lines.

Scalia wrote out a phone number, and an address. The address was on lower Fifth. "You call me, I'll give you as much time as you want. You're on television, right?"

"I'm practically adorable." I looked at the address, tried to remember if it was where Lea said it was. "These are for real, right, junior?"

Scalia cocked his head. "You always this sure you don't like people before you meet them?"

"Twice before. Mayor Koch and Gerry Cooney. No, three times. This television preacher named Endicott was in there too. I had 'em all cold before we shook hands."

"Oh."

"I'll be talking to you, probably with a camera and so forth, sometime soon." I got up. "Now two things before I go. They probably won't mean anything to you, because you're obviously on leave from the National Honor Society. But what the hell. One: It would be a lot easier for a guy to scare Sara Hildreth than it would be for him to scare me."

I motioned him to lean forward, and up. I leaned down a little. It might have looked in Knickerbocker's like I was going to kiss him goodbye. "The other thing is, if a guy were looking for ten thousand dollars, no reason to bother the coeds. I've got it."

I didn't wait for his reaction. I walked out the door whistling "Dark Town Strutter's Ball."

Finley is death on college students.

You should see me when the paper boy needs rousting.

CHAPTER

13

SCALIA and Sara and the money were all I really had. When Sara Hildreth wasn't saying "Knickerbocker's" she wasn't exactly my girl Friday. And contrary to legend, money doesn't talk. The money was in my apartment anyway. Sara was out at Patrick's Pub. Scalia and I were much closer than that, geographically if not ideologically. I pulled my Red Sox cap out of my pocket and pulled it down close to my eyes and walked across the street to an alley next to Lafayette Cleaners and decided to wait for Scalia to come out and do something interesting.

People kept walking into Knickerbocker's, some of them alone, men and women, college kids. I didn't know which one of them was Michael Scalia's date. I looked at my watch. It was nine-thirty.

At ten, I walked backward up to the corner of Tenth and bought a *Post*. Nobody gave me a second look. Maybe downtown they expect you to walk backward. The guy who did the back flip was normal. So was I. There was no reason for Scalia to notice me when he came out of Knickerbocker's, so I sat on the front step of the Lafayette Cleaners and read the sports section. I only buy the *Post* in the summer, and only then to read the Mets writer, Klapisch, who is the best baseball writer in town.

Scalia came out at ten-thirty. He was with a blonde. She looked to be in her early twenties. She was wearing a green miniskirt and a green-and-white striped blouse and heels. She was about Scalia's size, and much prettier. If I'd had my judge's scorecard with me, I would have held up a 10 for the compulsories: face, legs, body.

Scalia hailed a cab going west on Ninth. It was a small break for me, because when the cab made the right on University, heading uptown, it got a red light at Tenth.

I flagged an uptown cab of my own.

The world was not rich with opportunities such as this, so I grabbed the one I'd been presented with by the throat.

"Follow that cab," I said to the driver.

The driver, without looking back, said, "You shittin' me, right, doctor?"

It wasn't *The Thin Man*, but what the hell. I was dealt these cards, I'd play 'em.

EVERYBODY ended up at the New York Hilton. The cab with Scalia and the blonde pulled up in the circular driveway in front of the hotel. There were men in tuxedos and women with ball gowns in the cab line. I had my guy pull up on the left side of Sixth Avenue and wait.

Wait for what? I thought.

If Michael Scalia had an apartment, what was he doing at the Hilton?

I felt that was an excellent question.

The cabbie said, "We playin' Magnum Pee Eye all night, doctor? Or we comin' to the end of an episode?" He was black, with hair in shining ringlets coming out from the back of what looked to be a Borsalino hat. His license said his name was Devon Shire.

I watched the entrance to the Hilton and asked if that was his real name, Devon Shire?

"My ole man, he a real cutup," he said. "But if you really interested, my first name is pronounced De-VON, in case you was in danger of confusing me with the cream."

I got out of the cab.

"I'm not bolting," I said. "Just hang with me a second. I want to see where they went."

"Who went?" he said.

Scalia and the blonde had gone into the lobby. I went into the lobby. There were more tuxedos and ball gowns. No Scalia. No girl.

I went to the front desk and asked if there was a Mr. Scalia registered. A guy with a crewcut worked keyboard magic on his IBM.

"No sir."

"Is there a bar here?"

"There's two," he said. "Mirage, which is on the 54th Street side, and Pursuits, the disco, which is on the 53rd Street side. My advice, sir, would be to try Mirage, because you're not going to get into Pursuits dressed, um, like that."

I said, "Jeans?"

He shook his head sadly. "And no sports jacket."

"The Red Sox cap would have been all right, though?"

He laughed. "Don't ask me, I'm a Yankee fan."

I said, "Probably like the rest of them. Raised by wolves." I pointed at the computer. "You're sure no Scalia?"

"Sure."

I looked in on Mirage, an open lobby bar with all the charm of all lobby bars everywhere. They weren't there. I tried Pursuits. A bouncer who looked like he'd left Stallone school early said "Negativo" when he looked at my outfit.

I took the Red Sox cap out of my pocket and put it back on.

"Now?"

"Nope."

I took out a twenty.

"Bribe-a-tivo?"

Stallone said, "I'm good at reading people. Mom says it's a gift. This is not your kind of place."

"Did you happen to notice an oily-looking kid and a showstopping blonde come in here in the last five minutes or so?"

He said, "Nope."

Stallone was right about it not being my kind of place. I went and gave the lobby one last look, then Mirage. Negativo. Scalia and the girl were either upstairs in a room, or they had slipped past Stallone and were dancing the night away in Pursuits. I went back outside and got into Devon Shire's cab. There would have to be other nights for Michael Scalia and me.

"Sixty-eight and York," I said.

"Home James, and like that?"

"Yessum."

"You find what you were looking for?"

"Nah," I said. "But then who the fuck ever does, you know, Devon?"

He said, "Good point, doctor," and made a right into the night.

CHAPTER

14

BRYANT Gumbel was making fun of the Mets again. Gene Shalit said it's what he'd expect from a Cubs fan. Jane Pauley looked bored. Willard Scott seemed to be wearing a new three-piece toupee.

Jack Finley, my father, had put a towel over his legs so *USA Today* wouldn't smudge all its color all over his tennis whites.

I said, "You're the only person I know who reads the front section of that thing."

"They have a way of making even grief seem peppy and zippy," he said.

"It's like they all went to the Walter Winchell School of Investigative Reporting," I said. "The whole paper reads like a ransom note."

Andrew Jackson Finley had been asleep in the guest room when I got back from the Hilton. He'd been spending the month in our Bridgehampton house with the new love of his life, a former art director for one of the bigger Madison Avenue ad agencies. But there had been a dinner at the Players Club for one of his pals, Jack Whitaker of ABC Sports. Today there was a senior tournament at the West Side Tennis

Club he wanted to play. So at the breakfast hour, he was Fila-ed out: white shirt, white shorts with green-and-red trim, plain white socks with the small Fila emblem discreetly stitched at the top, new Fila sneakers that squeaked when he walked across the kitchen tile. All the white matched his hair. His Prince was downstairs in the trunk of his Saab.

My father had *USA Today*. I had the rest of the papers spread out on the butcher block counter between the kitchen and the living room. The Red Sox had beaten the Indians 10-6 because the new kid centerfielder, Burks, had stolen second and third in the bottom of the ninth, then scored the winning run on a sacrifice fly by Boggs.

"You see how the Sox won?" I said. "Sonofabitch, Burks can run."

My father said, "It only means management will hunt him down like a dog and shoot him. Or trade him to the National League."

"You haven't said anything about Kitten Something-Hyphen-Something," I said.

An arm came from behind the paper. His tea cup disappeared.

"Her name is not Kitten. Her name is Buffy Melville-Sloat." He rattled the paper theatrically. The color made waves.

"She still out at the house?"

"At this moment, I expect she's over at the Omni gym in Southamptom, beating up her Nautilus instructor."

"She's in good shape for a woman of, ah, her years?"

"She's in good shape for an Israeli fighter pilot."

He folded the paper and put it on the floor, took a damp paper towel from the coffee table, wiped his hands of the newsprint.

My father was getting more fastidious as he got older, and he wasn't Pigpen from Charlie Brown to begin with.

"Tell me more about your adventures," he said brightly.

I had told him about Julie Samson, her daddy, Lea, money, Scalia, Sara Hildreth, the blonde, the Hilton while we ate our eggs.

"I got two big questions, and I got secondary questions,"

I said. "What was Julie Samson mixed up in? That is the first big question."

"And the second question is whether or not young Scalia was mixed up in what she was mixed up in?"

I said, "I don't think the question will be phrased that way in the lightning round, but yes. You think I should stay on Scalia?"

He squeezed the last tea out of the bag. "Yes, I think you should. But make it a softer play when you see him next. And if you do continue to follow him, and investigate him, do it with quiet feet."

I said, "Quiet feet."

"No taps." He sipped the tea, flavored to orange mandarine. "You realize that even if it is dope, it doesn't mean Julie was involved, and it doesn't mean it's why she killed herself."

"I know."

"But you don't think it's dope, do you, sonny?"

"Negativo."

"Beg your pardon?"

"Never mind. A disco colloquialism. I don't know what killed her, but I'm going to find out."

Jack Finley looked at his antique Rolex, a gift from Buffy Melville-Sloat. He sprang out of his chair.

"I'm off."

I said, "Who are you playing first match?"

Jack Finley stopped in the middle of the living room, and brought an imaginary racket through for what looked to be a sliced backhand crosscourt.

"Tight Collar Flanagan," he said. "That dead ass."

LEA called before I left.

"Desmond Akeem Powell," she said.

"Good morning."

"Remember, you asked me to look into Desmond Akeem Powell?"

"I did indeed."

"Well, he's practically almost nearly flawlessly perfect. Born in Africa. Part African, part English. Graduated Stanford with honors. Master's at Berkeley. He's been at The Square three years. Julie took a course with him, South African history, last semester.''

''What do you mean, practically, nearly perfect?''

''There was some trouble two years ago. A girl, senior, accused him of trying to sell her a grade. The school ethics committee had a hearing, and President Ball ran his own investigation, and Desmond Akeem Powell was cleared all around.''

''He got an office?''

''Kornheiser.''

''He said he's been away lately in Africa. True?''

''That's the story. He's been away somewhere, anyway.''

''You got anything else for me?''

''Meet me at eleven. My room. I've got a couple of people for you to talk to, who knew Julie.''

I met Marty at the Hole-in-the-Wall deli at Fifty-seventh and First. He hadn't eaten breakfast yet. He was wearing a bowling shirt that read ''Tony's Texaco'' on the left breast. The cap was blue, with a gold ''S.''

''Cap?'' I said when I sat down.

''Seattle Mariners. New logo this season.''

I did not ask him about his date. He offered no information. It was like most mornings. Marty Pearl didn't look tired or alert, happy or sad, cranky or chipper, celibate or sated. Just hungry and waiting on the day, in a Mariners cap and a bowling shirt.

When his omelette came, I said, ''You ever wonder why there was no note?''

''Suicide note? Yup. All along. Even with a public death like that, you'd think she'd want to make sure everybody got the message.'' He poured ketchup on his plate.

''Where is it then?''

''I figured that whoever was in with her on whatever she was in on took the note. If there *was* a note.''

''She'd leave it in her room?''

''Yeah, but the cops would go straight to her room.''

''So we should maybe have Lea ask around Weinstein, see

if anyone remembers anything unusual the night she killed herself, or any time that day, really.''

Marty said, ''Smashing, old boy. What are we up to today?''

''You sound like Desmond Akeem Powell, who is simply wonderful, except somebody once accused him of selling a grade.''

''By George.''

''I tried his office, but he's not in. We'll have to talk to him at some point.''

''Repeat: What are we up to?''

''If we hustle, we can knock off the teachers from the other two classes Julie was taking this semester. A Professor Hilliard. Ms. Hilliard. American lit since 1950. And Professor Thorne. Economics. Then we meet Lea. She's got some people who'll go on camera, reminisce about Julie. We need some background.''

''Background, foreground, middle ground,'' Marty said. ''But I have great confidence in you. Delores says you're excellent at meandering. I agree. And you're special when it comes to stepping right into things.''

''You got all the stuff?''

''Yes.''

Marty motioned for the check. Etty, the bleached blonde, brought it with a smile as big as she was. I think she liked Marty. He gave her a ten and told her to keep it.

''I can't believe you haven't asked me about my date,'' he said as he pulled the van over to the right lane so we could get over on York and Fifty-eighth and take the FDR Drive downtown. ''Don't you have any interest in my personal life whatsoever? Am I just a big talented man behind a camera?''

''Tell me about your date.''

''No.''

PROFESSORS Hilliard and Thorne wasted our time. Or we wasted their time. Professor Hilliard had short hair, a bouncer's manner; Marty said later Dick Butkus would play her in the movie. She said she remembered Julie, but she didn't. She could have been talking about any woman at The Square.

Or in the universe. Professor Thorne was a cute little thing in tweeds too warm for the weather and rimless glasses. Truman Capote had willed him his voice. He said his class was a lecture with two hundred students, so he really didn't remember Julie, or her work. I wondered if his students remembered Thorne. Or if they could hear him in the lecture hall without Dolby Sound.

Lea's friends were women. One was named Alix Monroe. The other was named Maggie Frazier.

Marty said, "Monroe and Frazier?" when we were all introduced.

Alix Monroe said, "Is there a joke?"

Marty said, "Never to the Lakers."

Alix was from Greenwich, a junior with black curls and brown eyes and about fifteen pounds to drop before she was as pretty as she should be. I thought she might be a jock and then she told us women's volleyball. Maggie was the chattier one, an auburn-haired, long-legged, cheerleader type, wearing running shorts and the new Nikes with the clear plastic in the heel.

We were in the park. Marty didn't like the light in Lea's room, or the background. So we were in the park. We talked about it, and decided to shoot over my shoulder, the two of them sitting on a bench near the children's playground. It was quiet enough in that corner of the park, and Marty didn't mind the traffic noises.

Alix studied with Julie Samson sometimes, since they had Thorne's economics class. Maggie said she lived across the hall, and sometimes would hear Julie coming in at two and three in the morning, but she just assumed Julie was coming back from her boyfriend's.

I asked her if she meant Michael Scalia.

"No," she said. "This was after Michael Scalia."

I told Marty to stop tape for a second, and looked at Lea. She put arms in front, palms up. "First I've heard of it, and I thought I was going good. I guess I just assumed."

Marty started the tape again and said, "Go." I said to Maggie Frazier, "Julie Samson had a boyfriend after Michael Scalia?"

"Well, I assumed she did. She was coming in late like that two or three times a week. I'm a light sleeper. I'd hear her on the stairs."

"You ever ask her about it?"

"Once."

"What did she say?"

"Now that I think of it, it's odd what she said. I didn't look at it that way until this minute. But I asked her if she was seeing a new guy and she said, 'Don't you know a popular girl when you see one?' "

MONROE and Frazier left. Marty had me do some reverses. Reverses are the silliest part of television work, because what you do is try to make one camera look like two. It is one of the industry's milder dishonesties, right in there with the notion of something being "live on tape."

Reverses work this way: Marty shoots over my shoulder, camera on Monroe and Frazier. We do the interview. Lea, or Natalie, jots down the questions I ask in shorthand. I say, thank you very much to Monroe and Frazier. Marty goes and stands in back of where Monroe and Frazier were, and puts the camera on me now. I ask the questions all over again, only now I'm talking to my invisible rabbit.

After I ask the questions, we do a few reaction shots. Me nodding, me looking serious, me smiling, me nodding.

I always feel like a tool, or Robin Leach of *Lifestyles of the Rich and Famous*. Except he never seems to feel like a tool, he just seems happy to be in the Jacuzzi with Elke Sommer.

When we were finished with the reverses and the sparkling reaction shots, I said to Lea, "What does all that mean, can't you see what a popular girl I am?"

She lit a cigarette. "I don't know. It sounds like she was being sarcastic, I get that. But what was she making fun of?"

I said, "And who was the new guy?"

"Beats me," Lea said. She was wearing blue jeans. She plopped herself down on the grass and got into the lotus position. "I guess the best person to ask would be Sara. Maybe Julie was seeing the guy before Sara left school."

"Smashing, old girl," Marty said.

Once he got into a mode, he got into a mode.

Marty had parked over by Kornheiser Library. I helped pull Lea up, and we walked in that direction. There was a pay phone at the corner, next to the van. I called information, got the number for Patrick's Pub, used my credit card number to call Patrick's Pub. The guy that answered the phone said Sara Hildreth should be in soon, she was working the lunch shift. He asked if I wanted to leave a message, and I said I'd call back.

"Are you going to see Michael Scalia again today?" Lea said.

"Yes on again, no on today. I want to talk to Sara first. She knows so much about where Scalia likes to go, I thought she might have a theory on what he was doing at the New York Hilton. I don't think he went to the disco. I think he went upstairs to a room, only I want to know whose room it was and why he needed it."

Marty said, "Could have been the blonde's."

"I know, I know. But I just didn't get the feeling it was hers." I looked at Lea. "Give me a cigarette."

She said, "But—"

I said, "I'm not going to smoke it, I just want to hold it." She gave me a Kent III.

"I think you're playing with fire," Marty said. "So to speak."

"I think better holding a cigarette." I leaned against the van. It was all right. Marty kept it cleaner than his toothbrush. Across the street in the park, a group of street kids, three black, one white, were rapping and break-dancing for money. They had drawn a crowd, which was rhythmically clapping along.

I hate rap. Rap has to be stamped out along with pesto sauce and self-serve gas stations and artificial turf. Similar threats to society.

But I liked the dancing. It reminded me of the way Elgin Baylor used to play basketball, only they couldn't hang in the air the way Elg used to.

I was watching the dancing when I saw the girl.

SHE was clapping along with the rest, laughing, rocking a little, so every couple of seconds, she was facing in our direction.

It was her.

"Sonofabitch," I said. "I catch a break. There she is."

"Who is?" Lea said.

I pointed across the street. "There, at the back of the crowd. Khaki shorts, halter top, bless her little heart, Michael Scalia's blonde."

"Son," Marty said, "it's the naked city. Filled with millions. I think you manifested her. It's being that close to smoking. It's made you delirious."

"The hell it has," I said, pointing. "That's her."

Lea was staring where I was pointing, squinting.

She said, "That's no blonde, sir. That's Lettie Schorr."

I turned. Lea had taken her sunglasses out of her hair and put them back on her face. "You know her?"

"We take two classes together. She lives in Weinstein. We're not pals, so I wouldn't know if she was going out with Scalia, but that's her."

"She a friend of Julie's?"

"I'd see them together. I assumed they did some barhopping together because they'd go out at night once in a while. I didn't talk to her about Julie because she hasn't been around lately. She's graduating, but I think she finished early or something. I just figured she took a break someplace, maybe the beach, before all the graduation stuff starts. Holy shit, Lettie's going out with that furball?"

"Furball?" Marty said.

Lea said, "I'm a coed. I'm allowed sometimes."

The rapping and dancing was coming to an end across the street. The tallest of the black kids collected the old fedora with the money in it. One by one, the four kids took curtain calls, dropping to the ground, doing one more 360 spin on their hands. They got four more rounds of applause. Then the crowd started to disperse.

Lettie Schorr walked diagonally across the park toward Fifth.

I turned to Marty. "You up for some ambush journalism?"

Marty opened up the back of the van and got the hardware. He attached the shotgun mike to the front of the Sony. To Lea he said, "I just don't see how working with Mike Wallace could be any more rewarding than this."

The three of us half jogged, half walked, and caught up with her just as she was passing under the arch.

I came alongside Lettie Schorr on her left, Marty made a quick move to her right, to get up ahead of her. It wasn't exactly cricket what we were doing. I didn't even expect to use any of it. I just wanted to see how scared she got.

"Excuse me," I said. I smiled. Jehovah's Witnesses go door to door with less warmth. She stopped. "I'm Peter Finley from Channel A. I'm at The Square doing a piece about the life and death of Julie Samson. She used to go out with Michael Scalia and I happened to see you going into the New York Hilton with Michael Scalia last night, and I was wondering if I could ask you a couple of questions on camera?"

She saw Marty then. She looked at him then back at me like we'd come strolling into her morning shower asking if we could ask her a few questions about it on camera. When she started to turn in the direction she'd just come, there was Lea Ballard, dorm mate. She wasn't surrounded really, nobody would have stopped her, but you could see she felt that way.

"Hi, Lettie," Lea said.

Lettie Schorr dropped to her knees and began to cry.

"Aw shit," Marty said, and pointed the camera toward the ground. "I hate when they cry." Lea knelt down next to her. "He just wants to ask you a couple of questions," she said. Lettie had been carrying a purse. She'd fumbled it. Things had spilled out. I put them back in, picked the purse up. "Don't touch that," she managed, grabbing the purse, and then convulsed into sobs. Lettie clutched the purse to her chest, Lea put her arms around her, Marty and I watched.

He said, "This way you have, meeting girls, it's a gift, right?"

We didn't shoot it. We just watched her cry. She stopped finally. But now her makeup looked like it had been spray-painted on. I saw she had scraped one of her knees when she hit the deck. There was a splash of blood. Lea saw too, and when Lettie stood up, she gently dabbed a Kleenex on the knee. When Lettie Schorr noticed, she made a shoo gesture, not much follow-through in it. It said, get away from me. I thought she might cry again.

Lettie didn't cry. She said, "Get away from me. I don't have to tell you anything about Michael and me."

I held up a cautionary hand, like a school crossing guard.

"I'm sorry we snuck up on you," I said. "We're bad boys. But I was only asking you about a date. How come the hysteria? You hiding something here?"

She focused on me. Her mascara ran straight down her cheeks in a straight blue line.

"I could scream," she said. She wanted it to be a challenge, but none of us reacted like she'd pulled a knife.

Marty casually hefted the Sony back onto his shoulder and said, "Stop or I'll shoot."

Lettie Schorr looked at Lea. "What are you doing with these bastards? I thought we were friends."

Calmly, Lea said, "Actually, we're not friends. We're just all part of Julie Samson's death now. You, me, Michael, Mr. Finley here, Mr. Pearl. You can tell us now about Michael and yourself, or tell us later. One way or another, he"—she hooked a finger at me—"is going to find out."

Lettie said, "You're a bitch, Lea," and Lea just nodded and said, "Yeah, I guess I am."

I said, "Scalia's got an apartment, you've got a dorm room,

how come you two had to go to the New York Hilton to warm your cockles and so forth?''

Cockles made Marty Pearl sigh.

"You think you know so much," Lettie said. "But you don't know anything about the way it is with Michael and me. You nosy sonofabitch."

"You didn't go there to warm your cockles?" I said.

Questioning is always linear with me.

"I'm going to tell Michael about this," Lettie said. She started to back away from us. "Don't think I won't. I'd like to see you try this with him. You'll be hearing from Michael about what you did to me."

I said to her, "We're going to have to do this again. I hope we can do this without me having to get the police in on it. Maybe you and Lea could talk about it when you're both a little more composed."

Police got her attention. "What do you mean, the police?" she said. She stopped backing up. Her eyes got big. They were pretty eyes, even with all the red around them. I wanted to tell her to lose some of the paint.

"Well, of course, they're still conducting their investigation, and when I tell them you're connected to Scalia, they might want to call you in for questioning."

That was it. She turned and half-ran, half-walked across the park, in what looked to be the direction of Weinstein.

I said to Lea, "You'll stay on this for me?"

"Sure."

Marty said, "The police? An investigation? They might have to call her in for questioning?"

I shrugged.

"So I lied," I said. "Send me to cable television prison."

Marty said, "You still planning on having dinner with Gus Dancy?"

"I think so. I don't know. I'm gonna go home for a while, think on all this. Scaring the shit out of coeds wears on a man after a while, saps his strength."

Lea smiled. "You've impressed the hell out of me. Sara Hildreth, she tries to run, but she can't hide. Now you get a first-round knockdown on Lettie Schorr. I plan on staying on your good side.''

Marty said, "He does tire a bit in the later rounds."

I said, "It's why Joe Louis knocked me out that night in '41."

Marty said, "You were ahead on points. I told you to stay away from him."

"It was ego, nothing more."

"You could've been the heavyweight champion."

Lea said, "You guys done now?"

"Pretty much," I said.

I TOLD Lea to be careful about opening her door. She'd been broken into once. It might have been Scalia, might not, but now we had given him a reason to be spiteful. I told her if she heard anything, call campus police, then call me or Marty. If she came into Weinstein at night, make sure someone was with her.

"You're serious, aren't you?" she said.

"I have these moments of acute paranoia, yes."

"You think he might do something to me?"

"Might. I am starting to get a crazy theory about all of this, and I want to walk it around a little bit. But while I do, you be careful, hear?"

Marty, as usual, said he would drop the cassette by Channel A. I told him to tell Delores I would call her when I got back to the apartment.

First Avenue was backed up all the way to the tunnel that opens out at Forty-ninth Street near Peartrees Restaurant. We used to all go to Peartrees on Sunday nights in the old days, because Shirts Hughes, the greatest bartender of the modern era, worked there. O'Rourkes always looked like an emergency room on Sunday nights, dregs of the weekend washing up. Peartrees was always livelier because of Shirts, so we went there, and reviewed the events of Friday and Saturday nights.

But then Shirts died suddenly, and I'd heard that Peartrees had changed hands a couple of times. I got out of the cab and looked in the front window. It was the same. At least it looked the same in the middle of the afternoon. I thought about going in. Then I saw a young woman sitting at the end of the bar with the same color of red hair as Lea, and I thought about our conversation at Knickerbocker's. And I thought about how much of my New York life had revolved around saloons, and decided that I wouldn't want to be in Peartrees without Shirts anyway. He was from South Philly, Shirts. He loved the Phillies and the Eagles and Joe Frazier and a sweet girl named Lenore.

I kept walking up First, past Allan Elsner's Bookshop and the Southgate Deli and the jewelry shop at 55th and First where I'd bought Jeannie her engagement ring and Call Cuisine, which was the Four Seasons of take-out places, and nearly as expensive. Take-out food is the number one sport in Manhattan. You put two people from Manhattan together, perfect strangers, and let them talk long enough and they will quickly get around to the best deli they know, the best Chinese joint, and which ones deliver the fastest.

There was nothing special about this neighborhood. It was just mine. Or had been mine. I lived a few blocks north and a block east on York, but my first good apartment in the city had been on Fifty-sixth and First, so I'd always blended the new area and the old area together. I took a right on Fifty-seventh, and passed Tony Roma's, which has great ribs. I wondered if Sammy Renick, the old jockey, still lived across the street. I would see him at Roma's once in a while, and he would try to tell me how many stories there were at the track, and what it was like when he used to race against Arcaro.

I took the left on York and passed the Fifty-ninth Street Tennis Club. Actually, it was only a tennis club in the winter. In the summer, they took the bubble down and the East Side Bar League played softball on the Har-Tru courts, right there underneath the Fifty-ninth Street bridge. O'Rourke, who managed our team from O'Rourkes, called it "Bridgeway Park." The bounces were terrible and the lights were worse than the bounces, but it was still a hoot to play baseball underneath that particular bridge, that sassy old New York broad.

I walked down the hill from the courts and then past the Cadillac place and the restaurant Meatbrokers and then into our lobby, which still looked like one of the Vietnam movies from a few years ago. The whole lobby was being done over, and it looked like workmen were everywhere. Ness Selmani, my favorite doorman, was in a heated discussion with one of the workmen, so I just kept right on going.

I got out of the elevator on 15.

The door to my apartment was ajar.

I put my satchel down, then crouched down and listened from behind the doorframe.

Nothing.

I gave the door a silent push, and then reached around to where I knew the baseball bat was, in the corner near the hat rack I didn't need. The bat was from Don Mattingly of the Yankees. He'd given it to O'Rourke, and then O'Rourke had given it to me as a Christmas present. He knew I hated the Yanks but loved Mattingly. I'd kept it near the front door ever since an unpleasant young man named David, carrying an unpleasant little gun, had gotten into the building through the service entrance and into the apartment a few years before. Jeannie'd said, "I know you're a tough palooka with your fists, but the bat makes me feel better when you're not around."

I got my hand around the handle of the Mattingly bat and slid it around the doorframe and dragged it back to where I was crouched. I put my best righthanded grip on the bat, stood up, took a nice cleansing breath, kicked my door all the way open and walked into the foyer.

Nobody in the foyer.

The only sound in the apartment was the ticking I knew was coming from the wall clock in the kitchen.

Master bedroom or living room?

Right or left.

Living room.

I went around the corner briskly and saw her there, and as I saw, I remembered a joke Lea had made a couple of hours before.

That was no woman on the living-room floor.

That was my wife.

I KNELT down next to Jeannie. She was breathing. It worked out fine. I started breathing again too.

With the best couples, both partners breathe. After the Duke of Windsor kicked off, you didn't see nearly as many photographs of him and the Duchess waving from the sides of boats.

I made a quick tour of the apartment, master bedroom, guest, the gym I'd fashioned out of the tiny third bedroom, both bathrooms, kitchen, closets. Nobody home.

I went into the closet in the master bedroom, got my old leather briefcase out from under the two Orvis duffel bags I use as suitcases, opened up the briefcase. The ten thousand dollars from Julie Samson's room, and the key, were still there. If somebody had wanted the money, he hadn't looked very hard.

Or maybe Jeannie had walked in on him. Or he had walked in on Jeannie.

Jeannie.

I got a washcloth from the bathroom, and ran some cold water through it, and brought it back into the living room. Jeannie had been on her side when I came in. Now she had rolled over on her back, and was making a sound that would have been in the groan family if it could have made it out of her throat.

I gently dabbed the washcloth over a great face. She opened her eyes on the second dab.

Jeannie Bogardus Finley smiled weakly, reached up with her right hand, touched my face.

She said, "Surprise."

THE left side of her jaw was beginning to be a traditional purple, somewhere between blue and red. Jeannie said it hurt, but nothing was broken, leave her alone, already. I told her to keep the Ziploc bag with the ice in it on the purple.

"And you can stop kissing my hair now," Jeannie said. We had moved to the couch. "And you can stop asking me if I'm all right. I'm all right. I could pop you like I popped the man."

I could see across the room that her Orvis bags were still next to the front door, along with her camera bag, which was big enough to belong to one of *Sports Illustrated*'s top men. Jeannie herself was wearing a blue shirt that had LEMON written across the left breast and khaki slacks with lots of pockets on them and Adidas sneakers with blue stripes.

There was a new bracelet on her left wrist. It featured different colored beads the size of rocks.

"How about cheeks and eyes?" I said. "Can I kiss them? Isn't that what Emergency Medical Services does?"

She smiled again. This smile moved closer to Jeannie status, the sort of smile that usually requires sunglasses.

"That's not all they do," she said. She put the ice on the coffee table and said, "Enough."

I said, "Tell me again about the man. Before he hit you."

He'd hit Jeannie. I'd have to meet this particular man, of course. I'd have to explain to him in the strongest possible terms that hitting Jeannie was something you really didn't want to do.

Jeannie heard me thinking about it. She did that. She looked at me, and saw me talking it over with myself, and she always seemed to hear.

"I am going to say this one last time. You are not allowed to get hysterical because I'm the one who got socked for a change. Rules are rules, sport. You always told me it was part of the job description. Same goes for me. You would've taken the punch if he'd surprised you. Besides"—she touched the jaw gently—"it's going to be a hell of a macho bruise."

"The other kids at school will be so jealous."

"Okay," Jeannie said. "Back to our story. I wanted to surprise you. I got into London last night, stayed at that new hotel near Heathrow, then took the eleven o'clock British Airways. Super Club. I like Super Club very much."

"Why not first?"

"*Era* was paying, goose." *Era* was her magazine. She invented it. She was still editor of it. I thought it made *Ms.* read like a Supergirl comic book.

"Anyway," she said, "I made a quick pass through customs, got into a cab, came home. If you were here, I was going to keep it simple. Ring the doorbell, you open it, tackle you, see if things got interesting in the foyer."

"Forward of you," I said, and kissed a spot above her left eye. "But probably effective, considering how naked I imagine your lust is."

"Don't use those suggestive words. I've been in the bush."

"You're going to finish the story?"

"I've told you twice. Are you trying to memorize it?"

"As a matter of fact, yes."

"You ever going to let go of me?"

"You got a problem, lady?"

She rearranged herself between left arm and left shoulder. "Remind me to write a letter to the mayor about Emergency Medical." She sighed. "I'm more angry than anything else. All hell was breaking loose in the lobby. What're they doing, building a new subway line?"

"I think so."

"I guess Ness hadn't come on yet. There was a new man working the desk. I smiled at him, he smiled back, I didn't see anybody else, so I just schlepped the bags to the elevator myself."

"Security at this building is starting to make me a tad cranky, I've got to be honest with you."

"The door was open when I got here. I figured you just hadn't latched it. I dumped the bags and did a full Robert Young like you always do."

" 'Margaret, I'm home'?"

"Right. Same dumb old thing. Only it wasn't Margaret. It was the guy in the cap and the limo outfit. He came walking out of the living room, calm as could be, and I said, 'Who are you?' And he didn't say anything, and he looked like he wanted to go, but I was standing between him and the door, so we just stood there and looked at each other." Jeannie looked up at me. "I didn't go to pieces, you know."

I kissed her lightly on the lips. "I know. It was then that you started to go for the Mattingly?"

"Yup. But when I turned, he saw the bat. He got there first. I gave him a pretty good shot to the side of his face. I left a scratch like a cat. Then I ran into the living room and looked for something bigger to hit him with. The house phone was out of the question. He followed me. He said, 'Lady, I don't wanna hurt you.' I started to tell him to stay the hell away from me, but then the sucker punched me. It was a right, I think. Down I went. It wasn't like *Hart to Hart* at all. They always gave Jennifer a little shot of chloroform in the old handkerchief on *Hart to Hart*."

"Hart to Hart?"

"You should look that good at Robert Wagner's age, Peter."

"You'd recognize him again if you saw him?"

"Robert Wagner?"

"Yuck, yuck."

"I don't know. He had the cap pulled down pretty low. And I wasn't trying to take a mental picture of him. He was shorter than you, and looked pretty sturdy, and was light on his feet. All I know is, I got him good on the cheek. It's going to be sort of dodgy for him to explain it away as a shaving cut."

I kissed her hair again.

"Obviously, he was waiting for me. If he's been here lately, he's seen no sign of you. He might not even know I'm married. I'm the one he wanted to pop. Unless he wanted the money, but it doesn't look like he rooted around for the money."

"What money?"

I ran down the events of the last few days.

"And the man didn't take it?"

"Look around. He didn't look. Or he comes in, taps a place, then has a maid service come in and cleans up after him." I got up.

Jeannie said, "I thought you weren't going to let go."

"I'm calling the police."

She said, "Nope."

"The guy got into my apartment, the guy assaulted you."

"I'm not answering questions, I'm not going to the station, I'm fine. My jaw works well enough for me to kiss you like this." She leaned up and gave me a kiss that had an exclamation point after it. "Besides, if the man is involved in what you're working on, you and Marty will find him, and I suspect you'll get the chance to defend my honor."

"You really feel fine?"

She nodded.

"In that case, I've got other ideas about your honor," I said.

Jeannie Bogardus Finley said, "I love it when you talk dirty."

JEANNIE was propped up against all the pillows at the head of the bed. She was wearing the top of my O'Rourkes softball jersey. It was No. 8, for Yastrzemski. It was all she was wearing. The bruise on her jaw looked about as dark as it was going to get. She said it hadn't bothered her while we'd found such a pleasant way to fight off jet lag.

I was lying at the foot of the bed, head resting on hand, watching her. Rosemary Clooney was singing Ira Gershwin through the bedroom speakers. I'd made us iced tea with orange slices. I'd pulled the blinds but some light sneaked through at the top and the bottom, so we knew it was still day and not night and probably rush hour outside where York spilled onto FDR Drive. Rush hour was no big deal, one way or another. I reached up with my free hand and ran a finger from her right knee to her right ankle, and back again. You couldn't go wrong with Jeannie's legs, one of the great tourist attractions in the United States of America.

"Is that 'Strike Up the Band' she's singing?" Jeannie said.

"By God, you've done it, you've named that tune."

"It sounds like a torch song," Jeannie said. She sipped some iced tea and made a loud ummmm sound and smacked her lips. The key was the orange. You didn't want too much lemon in it or too much sugar. The orange seemed to come in and mediate everything. "God, she's got a pretty voice."

"I'm a little uncomfortable with her doing singing commercials for bathroom tissue," I said, "but the wonder girls come and go, and she just keeps going."

"How many people besides your dad and me know you have both Rosie Clooney and Eydie Gorme tapes?"

"You forgot Ella."

"Ella doesn't count."

"I simply have more liberal musical tastes than almost anybody I know. I don't think it's incongruent to love Frank Sinatra and Frank Zappa."

"You don't love Frank Zappa."

"I know, but I needed another Frank. Can I have a sip of yours?" I sat up and she handed me her glass. I drank the last of her iced tea. Now I made an ummm sound and smacked my lips. I handed the glass back to Jeannie. The glass featured flamingos. It had to be a wedding present.

"Who gave us these?" I said. She couldn't find Third from Lex sometimes, but she could remember the Bogarduses' phone number from when she was three years old and she could inventory our wedding presents like a stock clerk. I had often accused her of being able to remember the womb.

She said, "Flamingo glasses? Jonathan Schwartz." Jonathan had the most civilized radio program in America on WNEW. If there could have been a Nobel Prize in Sinatra, Jonathan would have had it. He was also an unbalanced Boston Red Sox fan.

I said, "I wouldn't have figured Jonathan for flamingo

glasses, but I bet he's got Clooney and Gorme records I don't even know exist."

Jeannie stretched languidly, like a cat.

"I'm going to take a shower, then you're going to call Gus and tell him you're keeping the dinner date and you're bringing a showstopper with you."

"You got haymakered. You flew many hours today, after flying many hours yesterday from Nairobi. I think we should order in and get you to bed."

"If I go to bed early, I'm going to wake up at three o'clock in the morning. I want to go to O'Rourkes. We'll get there early, have a drink first, you can tell me more about Julie Samson and friends."

"*You* want to go to O'Rourkes?"

"See, I'm delirious. Go with it, Peter."

Jeannie hopped off the bed, pulled the O'Rourkes jersey off, and casually flipped it over her head as she walked toward the bathroom. I could hear her turn the water on for the shower. I closed my eyes and might have been easing into a short nap when I heard her say, "Hey."

She was dripping wet, standing in the doorway, framed by the steam, tanned and long-legged and home.

"Then again," she said, giving the wet black hair a shake, "I suppose you could call Gus in fifteen minutes."

"You're kidding."

Jeannie said, "Do I look like I'm kidding?"

You had to say this for my wife:

She could play hurt.

CHAPTER

17

"I CAN'T believe we're eating upstairs," I said.

Jeannie ignored me and waved at McGee, another downstairs regular eating upstairs.

She said, "McGee is upstairs. He doesn't seem to have gone into allergic shock."

"I should've brought my Ray-Ban's. My eyes are very sensitive to this much light."

Jeannie said to hush and drink my coffee.

"Not having an after-dinner drink is unlike you," she said.

"I just don't feel like one."

We were upstairs at O'Rourkes. *Upstairs at O'Rourkes.* It sounded like the O'Rourkes exposé one of the busboys would write someday. Jimmy had gone downstairs to check baseball scores. Gus Dancy was downstairs making a telephone call. The piano player, dressed in a tuxedo, was actually doing a very professional job with "Dancing in the Dark."

"You asked for my opinion and I'm giving it to you," I said.

Jeannie said, "I didn't ask for your opinion." She was wearing a Laura Ashley summer dress of a flowery print, and big silver earrings with blue enamel in them that picked out blue from the dress.

"All I'm saying is that he didn't need to have all the hanging plants. It's like eating in a greenhouse."

Jeannie said to hush, I was going to hurt Jimmy O'Rourke's feelings if I didn't stop acting like a baby just because all the tables downstairs were full.

Gus Dancy came back from making his telephone call. Throughout dinner, he had been the old Gus, telling stories, joshing O'Rourke about his study habits when O'Rourke would breeze by the table, doing hilarious sendups of the administration at Washington Square University. I was sure the bitterness and meanness I'd seen at his office was still there, it didn't go away in a day, but Gus was doing a good job of keeping it hidden or locked up or both.

"Sorry," he said. "Around the time of finals, I should carry a beeper for the distress calls from students." Gus looked at Jeannie.

"You sure that jaw doesn't hurt?"

Jeannie said, "If my husband hadn't mentioned it to you, you wouldn't have noticed it."

"We're trying to find the guy so we can set up a rematch," I said.

Gus raised his brandy glass to Jeannie in a toast.

"Beauty," he said, "though injurious, has strange power."

"Byron?" I said.

"Milton," Gus Dancy said.

I looked at him. "You're shitting me. Nobody can quote *Paradise Lost*. Nobody has actually ever even read *Paradise Lost*."

"You're absolutely right, old Finley. It's why I was quoting *Samson Agonistes*."

Jeannie clapped me on the back and said, "English major. And proud of it."

Gus lit up a Camel. He was wearing the same outfit he'd been wearing the day before, the same outfit he'd been wearing for twenty years, except he'd changed his work shirt for a festive Hawaiian shirt dominated by red.

He said to me, "How goes the investigation?"

"Colorful," I said. "But it doesn't hang together in any way I've been able to figure yet. Last night, I followed Scalia and a girl named Lettie Schorr to the New York Hilton and lost them. Today, I happen to run into Lettie Schorr in the park, and she tries to parachute off the world to get away from me. Now somebody gets into my apartment and socks my main squeeze."

Jeannie said, "Thank you for that. Main squeeze. That must be the Byron you meant."

"Anyway," I said, "I know I'm getting closer. I feel like I'm in a cricket match. My score keeps piling up, but I have no idea why."

"And you still don't know what Julie was doing to make that sort of money?"

"Nope."

"Where does a college girl get that kind of money these days, Gus?" Jeannie asked.

"It's a lot of money to hide under the mattress, isn't it?" he said.

I said to Gus, "Could I hold one of your Camels please?" Jeannie started to say something. I held up a hand. "Hold, not smoke. I've been clean while you've been away, I swear I have." Gus shook a Camel out of his pack and handed it to me. I tamped both ends and held it with my left hand, between forefinger and little finger.

"Lea says that Julie wasn't a doper, far as she knew," I said. "But dope is the only cash business I know about on college campuses these days."

Gus said, "Selling papers."

Jeannie said, "Term papers? Really?"

"Really," he said sadly. Deidre was across the room, leaning against the bar, having a smoke. Gus got her eye and signaled for another brandy. "Anyone else?" Jeannie and I both shook our heads. She was still working on her white wine. Unless she got zany, she went through one white wine per hour.

Gus said, "It is the high crime of college life. To me, it is like the violation of the honor code at a military academy, or point shaving in sports. And it goes on all the time. No one ever has any proof, of course. A student does work beyond his capabilities, but the paper is flawless, the footnoting is flawless. What does the professor do? Take the kid to small claims court? The professor grades the paper and moves on to the next student, the one who's done his own work.'' He picked up his voice again. ''Those that think must govern those that toil.''

I grinned. ''Byron?''

''Goldsmith,'' he said. ''It's not funny, actually. It is as bad on its side of the street as a professor selling grades is on the other side. The rosy world of academe, eh?''

Jeannie said, ''She could have picked up that kind of money—in cash—selling papers? Did she have that sort of discipline? That sort of mind?''

''Did she have that sort of mind?'' He smiled. ''Yes, she did. As I told old Finley yesterday, she was afraid of it, the way she was afraid of her beauty. Could she have made that sort of money? Certainly. The enterprising young woman would pick her clients carefully, make them ones who could afford expensive fees, and use them over and over again. Lovely Jeannie, there are many, many students at The Square and everywhere who are in college solely to please mummy and daddy.'' He took a bigger bite out of the Hennessy than he intended, and had to wipe his lips with the back of his hand.

''Sounds kind of wimpy,'' I said. ''You think that could have been the deal, some big paper-selling operation? Could Scalia have been the brains behind something like that?''

''I told you he is a shark,'' Gus said. ''It is not inconceivable that he had both the cunning, the help, the where-withal.'' He looked at his watch. ''I must be going soon. A late date for old Professor Dancy.''

''Gus,'' I said. ''Do you know a history professor named Desmond Akeem Powell?''

''The stringbean dandy? I do, old Finley. If he didn't carry himself with such great dignity, he would be an object of much more humor around The Square. As a lover of the language, I could listen to him talk forever.''

"Do you remember him being accused of selling grades a couple of years ago?"

"I do. I was shocked when the accusations were first made, frankly. Desmond A. Powell did not seem the type. But he was cleared completely, by all the reviews. Why do you ask this question? Do you know the dandy?"

"I met him. He and Julie were friends. I'm a very suspicious person. I just found out about the charges against him. Now I hear you talk about grade selling. And I get to thinking."

"He seems a good sort to me. I see him in the halls sometimes. And again, he was cleared. But you never know, do you?"

"Gus, how much time left before everybody but the seniors disappear? You understand. Before I'm left holding a box of money and a couple of cassettes that show me terrorizing college boys and girls like I'm Freddie in one of those stupid *Nightmare on Pine Street* movies."

Jeannie said, "Elm Street. And it was your idea to rent it, so don't try to pin the rap on me."

Gus smiled at us both. "She was always a bit formidable for you. In horse racing, I would say that you are both thoroughbreds, but she is Affirmed and you are Alydar, always a neck behind." He finished his Hennessy. Deidre, as if on cue, brought the check. I tried to get it. Gus Dancy beat me to it.

"Mine," he said. "I would have paid anything for an evening such as this. You two have brought me better days for a couple of hours." He counted out what looked to be a hundred dollars, stuck it over the bill on Deidre's tray. "What were you asking? Oh, about the end of another gripping school year at The Square. There are five more days of exams, then commencement, then goodbye." He bowed theatrically in front of Jeannie, kissed her hand. "So goodbye."

He walked across the room, shook hands with O'Rourke, who had been standing at the top of the stairs, leaning on the banister in a cream-colored sports jacket, smoking a Winston and, I was sure, feeling like he was Rick in *Casablanca*, waiting for Major Strasser and his buddies to show up so the floor show could start.

Jeannie said, "He is still so sweet and cool all at the same time. And a little sad."

"He is. He doesn't like getting older one bit."

Jeannie stood up. I could feel heads turn in the upstairs room at O'Rourkes. In dark movie theaters when she got up to get another double popcorn, I could feel heads turn.

She said, "Okay, bub. Enough with the talk. Let's go home and get out of these wet things."

Jet lag was obviously a foreign concept to her.

IT took the world traveler ten minutes from front door to apartment to sleep. Included in the ten minutes were getting out of Laura Ashley dress, brushing teeth, washing face, hanging up Laura Ashley dress, fixing glass of ice water and placing on nightstand, kissing her husband, telling husband, "I love you," hearing husband say, "I love you the most, J.B.," before her big day ended.

I knew there was something I'd meant to do, but couldn't remember what it was. I stripped down to running shorts myself, sat in the big chair across from the bed, and watched her sleep. I liked watching her sleep. She went through life looking like a homecoming queen and wisecracking with the big boys, but when she slept, she was all girl, face very intent, very young. She was busy. Jeannie remembered her dreams the way no one I'd ever met remembered dreams. She remembered them in Technicolor, with detailed dialogue and complicated plots, and she relished telling them in the morning, first thing, like the perpetual girl coming home and telling about everything that had happened in school that day.

I hoped she didn't dream about hoods in caps and limo outfits. I wanted her to dream of the lions she'd told me about in the cab home, and the way the monkeys woke her up in the middle of the night because they were happily peeing on top of the tent, and the way the sky looked at sunset from the front porch of the Norfolk Hotel, and the color of the flowers, and how close they got to elephants one day, and how the joke was that her jeep was the one that always got charged, and how she couldn't wait for me to see the pictures of just the grass, God, I wasn't going to believe the pictures, because the grass was gold.

I started to fall asleep in the chair. I stole into bed next to Jeannie Bogardus Finley. I don't remember what I dreamed about. I rarely do. Jeannie says I don't work at it enough. She's probably right. I just slept until the ringing of the phone woke me up and Lea Ballard was telling me that they found Sara Hildreth dead.

HEY found her body in Douglaston," Lea said.

I said, "Wait," pushed the hold button. Jeannie was still asleep. I got the phone on the first ring because I always did. I shut the door and went into the living room.

"Slowly," I said. I looked at the kitchen clock. It was 7:15.

"I heard it on the radio," Lea said. "It's an area the locals call Arleigh Beach, down near the Douglaston Dock. I think the man said Shore Road. Anyway, they're saying drowning, but they don't know for sure."

I said, "When?"

"Sometime last night. Early this morning, actually. That's all they said. I called the station, and what they used on the air was all they had."

"You said drowning? Murder drowning or accidental drowning?"

"They didn't say. Can I do something?"

"Get over here."

She said, "You mean get over there now?"

123

"Now." I hung up and called Marty and told him what had happened to Sara Hildreth.

He said, "On my way. You want me to pick up coffee and donuts?" I told him yes, and then dialed the number for the 17th Precinct. Mick Dunphy wouldn't be there, but they knew me at the 17th because of all the times I'd hung around Mick's office back in my newspaper days. I gave my name to the sergeant who answered. He said his name was White, did I remember him.

"Your old man helps out Dunphy, right?" I said.

"You got it."

"Listen, I hate to ask Manhattan a Queens question, but I'm kind of in a hurry. If somebody needs a cop for something in Douglaston, where's the nearest precinct?" He told me just a second, he'd get it, and came back on and told me the 111th, in Bayside, and gave me the number. I called it, identified myself, and told the Bayside sergeant who I was, where I worked, and could he tell me who was handling the death of Sara Hildreth.

"Detective Monaco. P.D.U. Which is the Detective Unit, which you probably know. You just missed him, matter a fact. He just left to go back over to Douglaston. Said he wanted to look around a little more. When Detective Monaco looks around, he looks around. You can probably catch him over there."

I told him I was coming from the city.

"The city could be San Francisco, you could make it, once Monaco starts looking around." He told me to find the Douglaston Club, hang a left toward the water, that was Shore Road, then just look for Monaco's car.

I was showered and dressed by the time I looked down and saw Marty's van in the street. He and Lea were leaning against it, eating donuts. Jeannie was still asleep. I wrote her a note that told her where I was going, why, not to answer the door unless she knew who it was, and that I loved her.

I went outside and closed our apartment door. I made sure it latched. Then I pressed the elevator button and wondered if anyone loved Sara Hildreth, college girl I'd forgotten to call before I went to bed.

I wasn't going to tell Detective Monaco of P.D.U. right away, but if Michael Scalia didn't have an alibi for last night, I was probably going to put a hole in his day big enough for Marty Pearl to walk through.

I REMEMBERED where the Douglaston Club was on West Drive, but I let Marty go past Richmond before making a left. We finally backtracked past the dock, heading back toward Northern Boulevard, and found Monaco's unmarked. Across the water, on the Cross Island Parkway, we could see cars in a crawl toward the Grand Central, and Manhattan. Marty got the gear, Lea helped him, and I walked down near the water to where Monaco was.

Monaco was built like a water bug. He was five-nine, five-ten, somewhere in there, but he was way over two hundred pounds, and the first question I wanted to ask was if he got the gray suit he was wearing at some Round Man shop. He had black curly hair and bushy black eyebrows and even a lot of black hair on the stubby fingers that held the notebook and the pen. He was crouched down in a matted-down grassy place littered with beer cans and cigarette butts and sandwich wrappers. I introduced myself, he did as much standing up as the Lord allowed him to do, we shook hands.

"You move early," he said. "That your crew?"

I grinned at him. "We don't think of it as a crew. We think of it as a small group of honest men."

"If it's a small group of honest men, one of your honest men dresses up in women's clothing."

"We've talked to him about that."

"Dunphy said you were in love with your sense of humor."

"You talked to Dunphy already?"

"Wilson radioed me after you called him. I had him find Mick. Mick said you were okay, or we're not having this conversation. Mick also said that no matter what you said you knew, you knew more, but you'd lie if I asked you."

"My father worked homicide in Boston for about a hundred years. I was brought up to think of the policeman as my friend."

Monaco stuffed notebook and pen inside the jacket of the suit and nodded. ''Mick said you'd tell me about your old man, too.''

- He started to walk back up toward Shore Road. I walked with him. Marty and Lea waited up by Monaco's black Taurus.

I said, ''What do you got?''

''I got a drowning is what I fucking got.'' As soon as he started talking, the pudgy hands got busy. I figured it was why he put the notebook away. ''Some guy comes down at four o'clock in the morning, wants to fish, the moon catches something back where I just was. He knows it isn't Bruce the Shark from *Jaws*. Kids come down here all the time once the weather starts to get nice. They party. We roust them out of here. It goes on all summer. He figured the girl comes out here by herself, went swimming, drowned. He dials nine-one-one, and pretty soon, I'm here with the deceased.''

''You don't think she went swimming.''

''Not with her clothes on, including shoes. And she definitely didn't put the bruises''—he reached up and grabbed his own neck—''on the sides of her neck.''

''Was she raped?''

''It's happened here, but we don't know yet. You know her, right?''

''I met her.'' I sketched what I was working on, told him about the great chase from Patrick's Pub. I didn't tell Monaco how she put me onto Scalia, because Mick Dunphy was right, I was constitutionally opposed to ever telling a policeman everything I knew.

''You got any idea who would do something like this?''

''No, sir.''

''That the truth?''

''Sure. Anybody in the neighborhood see anything unusual?''

Monaco pointed at Marty and Lea. ''You want to do this with your small group of honest men so's we don't have to do it twice?''

''Deal,'' I said. Marty got situated. I went with the hand

mike. I told Marty I'd just ask the questions, then do a quick stand-up to cover us in case we needed it later.

On camera I said to Monaco, "Anyone in this area see anything unusual?"

"Not that we've come up with so far. It was a foggy night last night, which meant, at least according to the people who live around here, that this Arleigh Beach area wasn't crowded with kids like it would be on a better night, or later on in the summer. Besides, it had to happen sometime after two, because Miss Hildreth didn't leave Patrick's Pub until one-thirty."

"You think she was murdered?"

"I think she was murdered."

"Do you have a suspect?"

Monaco looked at me. "I always try to get one before breakfast, it opens up my whole morning and then I don't have to miss my tee time at the club with my regular foursome. No, I do not have a suspect at this time. She finished work. She had a drink with the bartender and the other waitress. The bartender said, did she want a ride home? She said no, she was meeting someone. The next time anyone saw her, it was the man going fishing."

"The bartender have any theories about who the someone might be?"

"He did not. He said Miss Hildreth was not seeing anyone at this time, at least not that he was aware."

"But she was meeting someone?"

"That's what he said."

"She met someone down here and he killed her?"

"Or she met someone, left the someone, and for some reason came down here by herself in the middle of the night, and ran into a geek, and the geek killed her. It's gotta be one or the other. But that's just my opinion. What do you think? You've been around crime fighting a long time."

I said, "It's gotta be one or the other." Then I thanked him for his time. Monaco grunted and shrugged his thick body and said, "Well, yeah." I liked him. He was all cop. I told him I would keep in touch. Monaco said, "I'll look forward to that. I love meeting people."

He fished into his pocket and came out with the spiral notebook and a pen. "Gimme some numbers for you." I did. I asked him for phone numbers on the bartender and the other waitress, and he wrote them down in the notebook, ripped the page out, handed it to me brusquely. Monaco said, "Dunphy's your friend. I'm not your friend. You find out anything I need to know on this and hold it back, you'll wish you didn't."

"I don't think I'll say anything smart right here," I said.

Monaco smiled for the first time since I found him in the weeds.

"That's the way I'd play it." He stuck his hands in his pants pockets, put his head down like a fullback trying to make one yard, walked toward the corner of Richmond Avenue and Shore Road and then up to the front door of a brick house. He rang the doorbell. It was actually more a waddle he had than a walk, but I had a feeling that Monaco would somehow find out if I thought about him that way. So I didn't.

Some people are so tough they don't have to talk about it. Detective Monaco was that kind of tough. It didn't occur to me until later that I didn't know his first name.

I CALLED the bartender, named Brendan Connor, from a pay phone at the Douglaston station of the Long Island Railroad. He said he still hadn't slept, so there was no reason why he couldn't meet us at the Howard Johnson's on Northern Boulevard.

Lea got us all coffee and we drank it in the parking lot. I used the hand mike again. Connor wasn't the day bartender from when we'd come out to see Sara Hildreth. He looked like a male model. Broad shoulders. All kinds of jaw. Nose with a little bend in it, so as not to make him too adorable. Blue eyes. Brown hair flecked with gray. The only thing that marred the picture was a scar, paled to white now, on his left cheekbone, and a couple of front teeth that needed capping, or a complete overhaul.

He was wearing a gray "Manhasset High" sweatshirt with the sleeves cut off and tennis shorts and white New Balance tennis shoes. He smoked one Marlboro Light after another.

Before we started, I said to him, "Sara came from around here, right? Do her parents still live here?"

He said, "They died in an automobile accident in January. On the LIE. They were driving to Florida to spend the rest of the winter down there. You believe that shit?" He drank some black coffee, winced, blew on it, drank a little more.

"Any other relatives?"

"Not that she ever talked about."

"She live in her parents' house?"

"They were renting an apartment when they died. It might have been over to Great Neck. Sara just had a little upstairs apartment over near the train station. I think that Monaco has already been there."

Marty said, "Ready, boys?"

On camera, Brendan Connor told me pretty much the same story he'd told Monaco. It had been a normal night of work, getting busy late. Sara Hildreth had gotten a phone call earlier in the evening, from a man.

Me: "He give a name?"

Connor: "No."

When the last customer left, she and the other waitress finished cleaning up and then the three of them had a drink, like they always did. Connor asked Sara if she needed a lift. She said no, she was meeting someone.

Connor: "I said, 'At this time of night?' She said, 'I'm going to have to talk to him sooner or later.' And Kitty— she's the other waitress—said, 'Wait a minute, who's *he*?' And Sara said, 'No, no, it's not like that.' "

Connor said Sara was the first to leave. Neither he nor Kitty noticed if she got into a car or in which direction she walked. The next thing he knew, it was Captain Monaco on the telephone.

"She was usually pretty nervous about things in general," Brendan Connor said. His big hands shook as he lit another Marlboro Light. "Lately, she got the jumps every time the bar phone would ring. But last night, she was pretty calm. As she was leaving, she said to Kitty and me, 'You guys take care of yourselves.' We just sort of waved and kept talking. But don't you think that was a funny way to say goodnight?"

* * *

"SARA was scared of Scalia," I said.

We were on the ramp leading to the tollbooths at the Midtown Tunnel. I was in the front seat with Marty, Lea was in the back. Marty was listening to WNEW. Mel Torme was singing something that would have sounded a lot nicer without all the scats.

Marty said, "Be bop a doo bop, cock a doodle doo." He had his aviator sunglasses down at the end of his nose. The cap of choice was black, and had "Newport Jazz Festival" written above the bill. "You think Cole Porter wanted all that be bop a doo bop, cock a doodle doo in there?"

I said, "You're not listening."

He said, "You're not talking to me. You're thinking out loud. There is a profound difference."

Lea put down her *Newsday* and giggled.

"It all keeps coming back to Michael Scalia," I said. "He went out with Julie Samson. He scared the shit out of Sara Hildreth. He knows I have the money. I ask this Lettie Schorr about him, I bring her to her knees. Literally. Scalia denies he talked to Sara when I know he talked to Sara. He could have broken into Lea's room, or had someone break into Lea's room. He could have hired somebody to get into my apartment and hit my wife in the jaw. Gus says he's a shark. Something funny went on at the Hilton, I just don't know what."

Marty said, "What about the Desmond Akeem Powell angle?"

"Angle?"

"Slant?" Marty said. "You know what I mean."

"I keep calling him. He isn't in his office. I've called his apartment a couple of times, gotten his recording. He hasn't called me back. I'll get to him. It's probably a reach with him and Julie and grade selling, but I'll ask anyway."

We got to the booth at the head of the Exact Change line. Marty tossed a token into the basket. Marty always had tokens. I thought it streamlined life immensely to always be in the Exact Change line.

I said, "I'm still socking it in on Scalia."

"You want to go visit him by yourself, or you want company?" Marty said.

"What about me?" Lea said.

"You're out," I said. We were in the tunnel. Marty switched to a cassette. It was Fred Astaire. He was singing, "Who's Got the Last Laugh Now?" Marty said, "You know why all the great composers wanted Fred Astaire to sing their songs?"

I said, "No cock a doodle doo?"

"Exactly. You want me to come with you or not?"

"Would you mind waiting in the car? If it turns out he was the one who hired the sonofabitch in the limo cap, and comes clean about it because it's the gentlemanly thing to do, I want him to be clear it's a fair fight when I get ungentlemanly."

"He's gonna look funny on television with a black eye," Marty said. He angled right as we came out of the tunnel, then left toward Third.

Scalia lived at the corner of Fifth Avenue and Ninth Street. The building was the old Fifth Avenue Hotel. Next to the lobby entrance was a restaurant, 24 Fifth Avenue.

Lea said, "Maybe I could go back to my room and have lunch ready for when you guys finish with the he-man work." She clasped her hands together in front of her, and batted her eyes as she looked at me. Nervous Nellie. That was the act.

"Don't be that way," I said. "That sort of cheap sarcasm makes you, I don't know, like—"

"Me and you," Marty said.

"What he said. I'd like you to go back to The Square and find out if any other women that you know, or Julie or Sara might have known, have left school suddenly in the last few months."

"If they have?"

"See if you can ask around, find out if there were any unusual circumstances."

"Okay."

"When's your last exam?"

"Tomorrow."

"I'll call you later in your room while you're studying, and tell you if you missed any good parts."

She walked away. Halfway to the corner of Eighth, she turned around.

"How did Natalie take it when you guys kept sending her away all the time?"

I yelled, "Very, very badly." She smiled and kept going. I think she felt better. Marty and I watched her go, head high, arms swinging, hair blowing back over her shoulders in the slight breeze that blew up Fifth from the direction of the arch, and the park. I didn't know what she was like drunk, but I liked her fine sober.

Before she crossed the street to the arch she turned and gave us one more big wave, as if she knew we were watching. "Two of those are dead, you know," Marty said.

"I know."

"It's no endangered species, but you shouldn't lose two this way the same month."

"I agree," I told him, then I walked into the lobby of the old Fifth Avenue Hotel. The concierge desk was to my right. The man behind the desk had a name tag that read, "Mc-Kelvy." It should have read, "St. Nick." His uniform was red, his face was round and pink, he had a full white beard and button blue eyes. I asked for Scalia.

"What apartment?" It was one of those brogues that could have been Scotch, Irish, English, or Peter Jennings on *World News Tonight*.

"Don't know."

He checked his chart and said, "Nine-F, but now that I think of it, he went out early and I don't think I seen the lad come back."

"Why don't you ring anyway, if it's not too much trouble."

He picked up his house phone, punched out a number, waited, hung the receiver up smugly. "Like I said, not there. If I ain't seen the lad, the lad ain't here."

I went back out to the van and told Marty. "No reason for you to wait," I said.

"I don't mind waiting. I actually think of life as waiting, with stuff thrown in."

He moved the van across the street and down a half block

to a meter. There was a bus stop near the corner of Tenth from which we could watch the entrance to Scalia's building. Marty went over to a deli he knew on Sixth and brought back sandwiches and some newspapers. Sara Hildreth had died too late to make the late editions. We ate the sandwiches and read the papers and then talked about the designated hitter rule, which Marty had decided he liked. I thought it was one of the few polyester parts of baseball. I tried in vain to get him to tell me who he was dating. I did the *Times* crossword in twenty-nine minutes. I asked him if he thought I drank too much sometimes. Marty said, "I don't, but if you even ask that question, then you probably do." I asked him how he knew that and he said, "I read it in a book." I called Jeannie and got the answering service. It was a good time to check for messages. There were none. About four o'clock, Marty went and got coffee and some chocolate chip cookies from Balducci's.

It was a pleasant afternoon at the bus stop. Marty updated his list of famous people you thought were dead, but weren't. The only name I could add was Maximilian Schell after he told me Randolph Scott had, indeed, gone over to the other side of the street. Marty said, "Frank Capra," but neither one of us was sure what side of the street Capra was on. Michael Scalia never came home.

Sometimes life is waiting without any stuff at all thrown in.

AT six o'clock, Marty stood up and stretched and said, "We going to eat dinner here?"

"No."

"We going to stay much longer?"

"Couple of minutes." I went back to the pay phone, called Jeannie again. Still not home. I told myself it was nothing to worry about, but left a message that if Mrs. Finley came back and checked the messages for the first time in our married life, to please tell her to wait at the apartment, I was on my way.

"You want messages, darling?"

"Sure."

"Some girl named Lea Ballard called three times, every half hour the last three. I s'pect you call over to the office, you'll have some messages from her there, too."

I called Lea. She sounded out of breath.

"What happened?" she said.

"I did the *Times* crossword in twenty-nine minutes."

"Well, then," she said. "The girl you left behind has more news than you have."

I told her to give, I'd done all the waiting I was going to do for one day.

"Nobody interesting left school lately, but somebody left school today."

I sighed and said, "Lettie Schorr."

Lea said that was her line.

"IS this like a stakeout?"

Lea had walked back from The Square. Actually, she had jogged back. Her hair was in a ponytail, and the rest of her showed my instincts about her had been sparkling. No designer running clothes. Cut-off jeans, plain white T-shirt, beat-up tennis shoes that looked like they had belonged to either Lenglen or Helen Wills Moody. No headband. No runner's watch.

Lea sat down on the curb. "Lettie left this morning. Martha Byrne, lives across the hall, saw her. Lettie said she was done with exams, and she'd just decided to go to Europe for a while. Said she was flying to London this morning, as a matter of fact. Said it was a crazy, spur of the moment thing."

Marty said, "Crazy."

I said to Lea, "Is she rich? Her parents, I mean. She can just up and be spur of the moment and fly to London as soon as she finishes exams?"

Lea said, "Funny you should ask. I had them pull her record. Told the biddy at the records office I was doing a term paper on demographics at The Square. Her father is a lawyer in Syracuse. I called him."

"What did you tell him?" I said. A thin, elderly looking man and an elderly woman three sizes bigger than the man walked into Scalia's building. The man was trailed by a poodle.

"I told Mr. Schorr that I was a friend of Lettie's and that crazy, spur of the moment gal had left her checkbook behind in my room last night when she was settling up for some books I'd bought for her, and should I mail it to him or what?"

I said, "Neat."

Lea stretched out her legs and touched one toe with both hands, then the other. "Anyway, I asked him how long she'd been planning this trip. He sounded a little miffed, soon as I mentioned it. He said she just called up him and the missus—he called her 'the missus'—last night and said she'd saved up all this money, and she was going. Mr. Schorr said she always did what she wanted anyway, why should she change now? That was that. He didn't ask me what's the matter with kids today. I called British Airways and Pan Am, they're the only two with day flights to London out of Kennedy. She was on the ten o'clock British Airways."

"Two dead, one in Europe, for you folks keeping score at home," Marty said. He bit off the end of a cigar, spit it into Fifth Avenue, lit it, and leaned back, all the time watching the entrance to the old Fifth Avenue Hotel. Lea kept stretching. When I tried to do that, my football knee raised itself up and delivered Martin Luther King's "I Have a Dream" speech.

I gave a yank on Lea's ponytail and said, "You done good. Tomorrow, you may concentrate on your studies." She stood up and kissed me on the cheek, and kissed Marty on the cheek. "Television is my life," she said.

I walked across the street. The new man behind the concierge was named Valenzuela. He had mocha-colored skin and spiked hair that had cost him a lot of tip money and one gold tooth, right of center.

I took his message pad and wrote down my phone number. I took a fifty out of my wallet and handed it to him.

"You know Michael Scalia?"

Valenzuela said, "He is now like my brother, I feel so close to him when I see him." It was somewhere between *him* and *heem*.

"The minute he comes back, you call me. If you get the service, leave the number here. But keep calling me. If I go out, I'll give the service a number where I can be reached."

Valenzuela smiled. I always had been fascinated by gold teeth. I wondered if there was one gold dentist on West Forty-seventh in Manhattan, in the row where all the jewelry shops were, so busy you had to wait six months just to get an appointment with him. "You gon to hear from me. I feel like I scratch out the right nombers today, win instan' cash."

I said, "If I get down here before Scalia goes back out, I am going to give you another fifty dollars, Valenzuela. I don't mean to be crass about our relationship and define it in monetary terms, but what we are talking about here is the potential for a one-hundred-dollar banner day."

"In that case, I tackle my brother, he come across the lobby too fass."

"I'm glad we understand each other. You got any change?"

Valenzuela said, "Huh?"

"I need quarters."

He opened the drawer. "People need 'em for the lawnry," he said. "How many you need?"

I took twelve, gave him three dollars in return. I went back over to the bus stop and dismissed the troops. I called British Airways and asked how many other airlines had night flights to London. The woman gave them to me. I started dialing.

I wanted Michael Scalia in New York, geographically desirable.

I did not want Michael Scalia in London, taking in Lord Nelson and Big Ben and the Beefeaters and the rest of the sights with Lettie Schorr on his arm, wondering whether they should go to Rules Restaurant before or after the theater.

I FOUND Jeannie napping in the bedroom when I got home. She was on her side of the bed, on top of the quilt, pillows barricaded all around her. I found her note taped to the bathroom mirror.

Mr. Finley,
     I was going to go shopping. Then I decided to go over to *Era* and take a forklift to back mail. I went to *Era* and jet lag tried to give me a bigger knock on the head than The Shadow did. I begin to fade even as I finish this cute note. Wake me when you want to dine, unless you have other ideas, big boy.

                              Your darling dumpling

P.S. I turned the phone off and let the service take the calls. Don't send me to the wife gulag.

I looked at my watch. It was after seven. There was no reason why a man couldn't have one civilized drink before dinner in the privacy of his own home, even Lea Ballard couldn't object to something like that. I took a quick shower, got into an old white buttoned-down Brooks Brothers and my most faded jeans, fixed myself a light Jack Daniels and water with extra ice and put Brokaw on the television. It is what you do at seven o'clock.

Channel A had moved its nightly news from seven-thirty back to seven, but the two anchors looked like Ken and Barbie; I couldn't watch them without wanting to dress them up in different outfits. When we hired them, I told Charlie Davidson that very thing. The little guy sighed and said, "Actually, we got them from an affiliate we found on top of a wedding cake."

It wasn't his call, hiring them. Charlie hated twinkies. The new owner of A, a woman named Fay Zausner, picked Ken and Barbie herself, and didn't want to hear anything about it from Charlie. Fay's late husband, Al, owned a lot of small UHF stations in the midwest, then parlayed his little stations into a cable empire after the Cable Boom happened. Charlie had liked Al Zausner, liked him a lot. Charlie thought somewhat less of Al's widow. After every meeting with Fay Zausner, Charlie would come into my office and give me a one-sentence, sometimes a one-word, review.

"Vanna wants more game shows," Charlie would say. He called her Vanna.

Or: "Vanna wants an aerobic talk show."

Or: "Up-fucking-scale."

Or (imitating an amazing manner of speech that featured both a locked jaw and a frozen upper lip): "We may not like it, Charlie, but those shopping networks are the future. You know what I'm saying?"

Fay Zausner punctuated just about every thought with, "You know what I'm saying?"

I sat down and watched Brokaw. He was on the road that week, doing the *Nightly News* from Seattle with the Space Needle as backdrop. As usual, he had a perfect dimple in his tie, brought perfect pitch to stories from the top of the show to the bottom.

I kept waiting for him to say, "Peter Finley, normally a crack investigative reporter for New York City's Channel A, once again reported new leads on the Julie Samson suicide, but no fucking progress. . . ."

Lettie Schorr had left the country. Lettie Schorr must have had a stash of her own. Unless she was Michael Scalia's darling dumpling. And if that was the case, then they were in Europe together, and Scalia wasn't holding whatever I had together anymore, because he was gone. None of the major airlines listed a reservation for an M. Scalia, but that didn't mean anything, the reservation could have been in another name. Or he was going tomorrow night. Or the next night.

Or he wanted to negotiate that rotary on the Champs-Élysées for a couple of days, then he was going to London.

Or Lettie left because she was scared of Scalia. Or somebody. Or something. But she had to make plans to leave before she found out about Sara Hildreth, because she left the same morning Sara Hildreth's body was found.

Out loud I said, "Did Scalia kill Sara Hildreth?"

I sipped my drink. Brokaw was leading into a "Special Segment" feature about sharks. It made me think of Gus Dancy's description of Scalia.

I pulled my notebook out of my satchel, found Arthur Samson's phone numbers, called his home. He picked it up himself on the third ring. He said hello, I said it's Finley, he said, what can I do for you?

"I'm sorry to bother you at home, but I want to ask you a question."

"If it's about that interview we discussed, I still don't think so." I pictured him in his suit, for some reason.

"It's not why I'm calling. Have Julie's things been delivered to you yet?"

"No, they haven't. I thought they'd be here by now, but no, the school hasn't sent them. Why?"

"Nothing serious. I went through the stuff once, but I've reached a dead end in my story, and I thought I might have missed something the first time that might make more sense to me now. I'm going to take another look."

Samson said, "Are you any closer to knowing . . . why?"

"I am, and I'm not. I'd rather not talk about it on the telephone."

He said, "As you wish. Is that all?"

"One more thing. When you spoke to Julie before your trip to Los Angeles, and you asked her if she needed money, what did she say?"

"You want her exact language?"

"I want to know, what was her attitude about money?"

There was silence at Samson's end of the line. Finally, he said, "You know, she laughed. And I asked her what was so funny and she said, 'Money is funny.' "

We hung up. I went outside to the terrace, sat in one of the new lawn chairs Jeannie had bought before she went to Africa, put my feet up on the railing and watched dusk start to fall over the river like a big old quilt. I finished my drink after a while. I thought about having another and decided it would be a mistake on an empty stomach, or maybe just a mistake. I called Lea's room at Weinstein instead. No answer. I left a message on the recorder I'd made her buy, and told her I'd probably be in Julie Samson's room when she came back. I looked in the bedroom. Jeannie was on her back, smiling, probably dreaming about big, sleepy cats. I put on socks and sneakers. I made sure Julie Samson's key was still on my key chain. I went downstairs and gave a wave to Lenny Morrissey and hailed a cab and told the driver to take FDR Drive South and get off at Fourteenth Street.

If they gave frequent flyer miles for going from uptown to downtown, I was pretty close to winning that trip to Hawaii.

The door to Weinstein 608 was locked. I opened it with the key I hadn't returned to the woman at the registrar's office, and turned on the light.

The room looked the same as when Marty and I left it, and needed some air. I walked past the boxes and to the window, opened it, looked out and saw night now, not dusk, settling on Washington Square Park. It was like looking at an old black-and-white movie. I remembered the May night in the long-ago when I had looked down and there was O'Rourke, carrying a cooler, yelling up at my window. He had finished the last exam he was ever going to take that didn't involve an eye chart and parallel parking.

"Scribe," he yelled. "I have passed in my last blue book. It is time for us to celebrate."

He had beach chairs with him. He set them up on the grass nearest Garibaldi, and turned on his ancient Zenith transistor to a Yankee game against some forgotten opponent, and we sat and drank Budweiser beers out of cans and toasted just about everything worth toasting after four years at The Square. By the time we finished the case of beer, we had reached that point where a weepy pledge of love and friendship was required, and a hug. So we were both a little drunk and a little unlucky, because Jeannie came by during the hug part, looking for both of us.

"Jimmy, you dance any way you want to," she said to O'Rourke, "but I wouldn't let him lead."

She said she was cutting in on O'Rourke, and he found some slow music on the radio, and Jeannie and I danced under the stars in Washington Square Park.

There had been a lot of memories like it the past week. I opened Julie Samson's window and reluctantly let go of another one, then turned back to the boxes, and set to work. I went through clothes again, and the shoe boxes, and all her books, opening every one to see if there was some slip of paper hidden in one of them that might have one shred of relevant information, something that a guy wouldn't feel ashamed to call a clue.

I went through a shoe box filled with facial creams and makeup and brushes and the like. There were some earrings in there and a locket I hadn't paid much attention to first time through and a couple of rings. The locket looked like an antique. It looked like the kind you opened. I tried. It didn't open. Then it did. There were two photographs inside. One was an old black-and-white shot of a woman; mother probably. The other was a color shot of a little girl in a white lace dress and a little boy in a white suit, standing awkwardly in front of a brick home. Julie and the dead brother? The sister and the dead brother? The pictures made me very sad. I reclasped the locket, placed it carefully in the breast pocket of my white shirt. When I saw the father, I would give him the pictures of the wife and family he had lost.

Finally, there was one more big box, filled with the nonsense and junk you accumulate in college. Matchbooks littered the bottom of the box, from Chumley's and Googie's and Pete's Tavern and the Astor Bar and "21." An unopened package of Certs. Certs with Retsyn. Ashtray from the Astor Bar. Faded American Express receipt from Tiffany's. Two from Saks. Two from some store called Pegasus. I stuffed the matchbooks and ashtray and receipts in my pocket.

I was sitting on the floor, facing the window. Later on, I couldn't remember whether I had latched the door behind me. I guessed that I didn't. It was my week for unlatched doors. The light went off and I said, "Hey," and turned around and started to get up and saw two of them coming for me like shadows in what light came from outside.

I didn't even get my hands up. I could make out a little one and a big one and they both knew what they were doing. They separated. I tried to make a break right up the middle. A leg came out and I started to go down, and then the first punch came, a chop to the side of my head. I went down on my hands and knees and tried to scrabble away from them like a crab. One of them just jumped on my back and took me all the way down, and turned me over and then somebody kicked me hard in the kidneys. I groaned and reached for my side and then one of them was on my chest. I got slapped on one side of my face, then the other. Repeat the process. I tried to say, "What do you—" and that was as much as I got to say before they turned me over on my stomach again, and I could feel them tying my hands behind me, and then some kind of blindfold being fastened roughly over my eyes.

Back over on my back. I could taste blood at the corner of my mouth.

"If you'll just tell me what the fuck you want," I said, and somebody slapped my head to the side. "Is this about Scalia?"

One of them said, "Shuddup." Sighed. Said, "We keep telling you, but you don't want to listen. You are very stubborn, boy. It is time for you to leave this shit alone."

He was to my left. From my right, the other one grabbed my hair and pulled my head back.

One to my left said, "Next time, something will happen to one of them girls a yours. You understand? Nod to let me know you understand." The other one let go of my hair, and I nodded.

One to my left said, "I'm gonna ask you a question, and I want you to tell me the truth."

I nodded. I get a good thing, I stay with it.

"Did you or that college girl lives here take anything out of this room? Nod."

I did.

"What did you take out of the room?"

I said, "I took ten thousand dollars I found in a shoe box."

"That all?"

"A key. A key was in the shoebox with the money."

"You sure that was all? I been in your apartment, boy. I din't have time to search it, since I didn't know your old lady was going to be there. But I can get in and do it again if you're lying. You sure that was all?"

"That was all. Is it somebody's money? I'll give them back the fucking money."

I turned my head and spit out what tasted like blood. Then I tried to shift some weight, take pressure off the side where I'd been kicked. The one to my right shoved me back against the wall.

I said, "Is this about Scalia?"

"You just remember what I said. You are snooping around where you are not supposed to snoop around, and you have made someone unhappy because you don't get a message very well. You understand? Nod."

I nodded.

I said, "Can I ask you a question before you go, Shorty?" I slurred some at the end, because I could feel the corner of my mouth where I'd tasted the blood starting to swell.

One on the right giggled and said, "Shorty."

Shorty said, "What?" He was still to my left. His face was close to mine. His breath smelled like a garbage skow.

"You the one who hit my wife, right?"

"Sure, why not."

The other one giggled again and said, "Yeah, Shorty did it."

I said, "In that case, you better hope I don't ever find you in front of me with the lights on, you chickenshit little . . ."

From the left I heard, "Enough chitchat." From the right came the last shot to my head. It did the trick. The conversation had clearly started to drag. Finley went over, Finley went out.

CHAPTER

20

I WAS in an apartment. It wasn't our apartment, because I could see into our apartment. Like *Rear Window* time, right? Jeannie was sleeping on the bed, and the two men, one little, one big, the little one in the limo driver's outfit and the dumb cap, were checking the other rooms, one by one. They were in the living room, then the guest bedroom, now they were moving down the hall toward the master bedroom. Jeannie slept. I had to warn her. Yell at her, wake her up. Our apartment was just across the way. Bedroom window was open, Jeannie didn't like it closed when she slept. I tried to open the window where I was standing. Wouldn't go. Little and Big were in our bedroom now, one on each side of the bed. My window was locked. I unlocked it. I shoved it open. But then when I tried to scream out to Jeannie, tell her to wake up, to get out of there, the scream died in my throat, then the lights went on, and Lea Ballard was kneeling in front of me, taking the blindfold off me, saying, "God, what happened?"

I said, "Ouch, and so forth."

Lea said, "You can say that again."

"Ouch, or so forth?"

She had gone behind me, was freeing my hands. Shorty and the giggler had used tape they'd found on one of the boxes for my hands, a rag for my eyes. I was sitting underneath that window in Weinstein 608 that looked out to the park. I felt like I had been dragged behind a gypsy cab down Lexington Avenue, then dumped in a pothole.

Lea said, "I came back from the library and got your message. But when I came down here, the door was shut and the lights were out, and I didn't think to try the door. I started to go back to my room, then I heard you yell out, and the door was unlocked. What in the world happened to you?"

I told her. I told her it was the same guy who had gotten into my apartment, probably the same guy who had gotten into her room. And now he had a straight man.

"What're they looking for? I thought it was the money, but you say they didn't care about the money."

I stood up gingerly, an inch at a time, finally stopping with hands on knees. My side felt like a side is supposed to feel when it has been kicked like a can. I got all the way up, after a couple of months, went into the bathroom and urinated. No blood. I looked at my face in the mirror. It wasn't as bad as I thought. One side of my face was red from the slaps and I had a lower lip that had been pumped full of helium. I had a headache. But I would live. I didn't want to go on an outing with Shorty and the giggler, but if they'd wanted to do more damage, they could have done more damage. The message was more important than the massage. I would have to tell the singing telegram people about them.

I came out of the bathroom and said to Lea, "I don't know what they were looking for, in answer to your question. There is a chance they were looking for nothing, that the whole point has been to scare us off. You a little bit. Mostly me." I sat down on the bed. "Right now, I would like you to do two things. I would like you to call my apartment and if my wife has turned the phone back on, tell her what happened, and that I am fine. I will wait here while you do that. When you come back, bring me three of whatever brand aspirin you have that has the most kick to it."

She went out the door. I went over to the box that I remembered had the Wild Turkey in it. I uncapped the bottle and took a swig, wincing as some of it burned my lip, then again as it burned its way into my stomach. Then I took another, and put the cap on the bottle and the bottle back in the box. I would have waited to do it with the aspirin, but I didn't want to do it in front of Lea. The bourbon was like the ethyl-something that baseball trainers used when a ballplayer got hit by a pitch. It couldn't make the pain go away, but for the short haul, it did the trick as a numbing agent.

Always had.

I looked at my watch. It was ten-thirty. I heard Lea on the stairs. She had a glass of water, and a Baggie filled with ice. She said, "There is something funny going on."

"How so?" She handed me three Bufferin tablets and the water. I swallowed the Bufferin. Then I put the Baggie to the lower lip.

"I called your wife," she said. "She told me you should hurry home, the two of you could compare bimps." She reached into the pocket of green sweatpants and took out her pack of cigarettes, and lit one. "Bimps?" she said.

"Bimps are bumps."

"Sure they are."

"Didn't you ever watch Clouseau? He called bumps bimps."

She sighed. "Thank God we've got that settled. Now we can go ahead and finish the cattle drive and start a new life out west."

I said, "Give me a drag."

"You sure you want to smoke? You've been going good."

I reached out with my hand. She handed me the cigarette. It was low-tar and not a Marlboro, which meant it tasted like a burning Bounty paper towel, and I didn't care. The worst cigarette I ever had was great. I took another drag and handed it back. It would have gone better with the Wild Turkey, but you couldn't have everything.

"Anyway, Jeannie, she said you had two interesting messages when she woke up and checked the service. One was from Detective Monaco out in Bayside. He wanted you to know that when they got over to Sara Hildreth's rented room, guess what they found?''

"Somebody rifled it."

"You bet."

"I'll call Monaco in the morning, we'll go back out there. Other message?"

"Master Michael Scalia." She grinned. "You think there should have been a drum roll?''

I said, "No shit." My jaw was starting to hurt; it was from the punch that knocked me out. There was a little Kent III left. I gestured for it. Lea handed it over.

"He wants to see you. Says he has something the two of you need to talk about."

"When?"

"The message said he'll be home the rest of the night. You going over there?''

"I am, yes."

"Call first?"

"And spoil the surprise? Frankie wouldn't do it that way with Annette."

"You want me to go with you?"

"No. What time is your exam tomorrow?"

"Nine."

"Call Marty. Tell him I'll call Monaco in the morning, set up a time when we can meet him at Sara Hildreth's, probably around noon or just after.''

Lea said, "What are you smiling about?"

I said, "I think it's time for Michael Scalia to find out what it feels like to get a bimp on the head."

VALENZUELA was behind the desk at 24 Fifth. He had a transistor radio on the desk, and was listening to what sounded like a country song. I said, "Merle Haggard?"

It was a shot in the dark. After I get by Willie Nelson, they all sound like the old theme song from *The Beverly Hillbillies.*

Valenzuela showed me his gold tooth and all the white ones. "George Jones."

I said, "He could write a sad country song about the doorman who had an easy fifty and lost it."

Valenzuela took his teeth back, turned down the music.
"Mr. Scalia don come back yet." I told him to ring the
apartment, then act like it was a mistake. He did, then
slammed down the receiver. "That fucking Rico. I tell him
to watch the fron' door for two minutes, I gon to take a pee.
I tell him, watch for Mr. Scalia. I describe him, everything.
I come back and say, Mr. Scalia come in? Rico is watching
the girls walk by in their shor' skirts. He say, No-body like
him come in. I say, You sure, Rico, I can buy a ver' nice
present for Estrella with money I can make with one phone
call. Rico, he still staring out the fron' window, hoping more
shor' skirts come by. He swear no-body come in. I gon to
walk up to him later, smiling, and give his thing such a
squeeze, pee will come out of his eyeballs for a week, two
weeks, maybe."

"I'm going up," I said to Valenzuela. I took out my wallet
and gave him a twenty. Even reaching back for my wallet
hurt the kidney area. "Your story of loss has moved me in a
profound way. Tell Estrella I said hi." Valenzuela asked if I
wanted him to ring the apartment. I shook my head. He said
when I got out of the elevator, go right, it was the last apartment on the left.

"WHO is it?"

I thought about Shorty and the giggler and how they were
going to revolutionize the singing telegram business.

"Western Union."

I could hear him slide back the peephole on the door. As
he did, I put my finger on the tiny window. From behind the
door, he said, "What? You have your finger over the hole
out there?"

"Telegram. For Mr. Michael Scalia. Doorman said he
tried to ring you, the phone didn't work. Come on, man.
This is my last stop of the night. Open the door, so's I can
get out of here."

I heard the door being unlatched. The door opened. Scalia
said, "Hey, it's—" and before he got anything else out, I hit

him a straight left hand that snapped his head back and
crossed his eyes. I stepped right in behind it and grabbed the
front of his wine-red Polo shirt and grabbed him in the horse-
and-rider area with my right hand and backhanded him on
the left side of his face with my left, then open-palmed him
on the right side of the face. I still had hold of his shirt. I
pushed him through the entranceway and into what looked
like the living room and shoved him back on the couch.

Look sharp, feel sharp.

"I know, junior," I said. "Barbara Walters doesn't do it
this way, but over the last couple of days, you have officially
started to wear my ass out."

"What'd I do?" It came out in a whine. He was looking
at me like I was a pit bull. Touched his hand to his nose as
though the nose might explode if he touched it too hard.
There was some blood coming out of one nostril. "I think
you broke my fucking nose. You gone fucking crazy, man?
Come busting into my fucking apartment? I called you, ass-
hole."

I leaned down close to him. "Watch your mouth, junior.
I have had a very bad night." I looked around. "Kitchen
over there?" He nodded. I went in, found a clean washcloth,
opened the refrigerator, put some ice in the washcloth, came
back and handed it to him. "Put this between your lip and
your nose. That's where I hit you. If I'd wanted to break your
fucking nose, I would have." He did what he was told with
the washcloth.

"Why did you call me?" I sat on the coffee table in front
of the couch, facing him, staying on top of him.

"It's like I said on the message. We need to talk. I'm
getting ready to go away for a while, and I think we can help
each other."

"Going where?"

"Europe."

"With Lettie Schorr?"

He took the washcloth away.

"How do you know where Lettie is?"

"You're kidding, junior. You didn't see the thing about
her trip to London on the People Page of the *Daily News*?"

The area behind Scalia's upper lip bulged some. He was feeling around with his tongue.

He said, "Does it ever occur to you that you're not the cut up you think you are?" He got up, said, "I'm not going anywhere," walked into the kitchen. I could hear the water running, then him spitting. He came back without the washcloth. He said, "Are you through showing me you can beat me up?"

"Probably." My head was starting to hurt again. "I would very much like three aspirin and a cold beer."

"By the way," he said. "What happened to you?"

I told him about my madcap adventures in Room 608.

"I think you hired them."

Scalia said, "You think I need muscle?"

"One of them got into my apartment, hit my wife. One of them, or both of them, got into Lea Ballard's apartment."

"She the one Lettie told me about, lives in Weinstein, helping you with whatever it is you're doing?"

"Yes."

"I don't know who those guys are, but they aren't mine, you gotta believe me. Besides, if they were, assuming they were, what's to have prevented me from calling them, getting them over here right now and working you over again?"

"I'm not up to a high school debate. Maybe you still think you're a tough guy. Go get the aspirin."

I looked around. Michael Scalia lived very well for a college boy. The furniture was all No Decorator, Early American, Bloomingdale Expensive, in various shades of creme- and light-colored wood, but it had cost some money. There was a pine table in front of pine bookshelves, and two Matisse prints and a weave on the wall over one of the couches that hadn't come from Bloomingdale's, that someone had done by hand. The lamps seemed to have come with the furniture. There was a big dhurrie rug over the hardwood floor. I knew it was a dhurrie because Jeannie had picked out ours; I figured a woman had done the same for Scalia. The Fisher sound system was built around a big Sony television set, and there were big speakers in the four corners of the living room. I imagined the bedroom would be something to see, not Early American but Early Hef. Scalia was the type.

He came back with the beer, Dos Equis, and handed me three tablets. I looked at them. Only two. "Don't worry," he said. "They're Tylenol with codeine. You can buy them over the counter in Canada. I got . . . I have a couple of stewardess friends who bring them back for me."

I put the two Tylenol-with-codeine on my tongue, drank some Dos Equis, tipped my head back. These were the invigorating beer moments they didn't show in the television commercials.

"What do you give the stewardesses in return? Couple of grams?" Scalia sat down in a creme-colored chair. I was on the matching couch now. I must have wrinkled his Polo shirt, because he'd changed into a yellow Polo sweatshirt, and tennis shorts. If GQ came busting in for a shoot the way I did, the kid was ready.

"You think I deal? That's what you think this is all about, don't you?"

"This apartment part of your MacArthur Foundation Genius Grant?"

He said, "I pay for it."

"How?"

"We're getting ahead of ourselves." He walked over to the bar, reached into an ice bucket with silver prongs, put a couple of cubes into a glass, poured some Glenlivet over it. He carried himself like he was back in command now.

"Sara Hildreth is dead," I said. "I don't suppose you know anything about that, junior."

He situated his drink on a coaster. "Lose junior, or the conversation is over. You can beat me silly, I don't give a fuck."

"I went out to see Sara Hildreth a couple of days ago. Or maybe it was yesterday. Sara Hildreth was scared to death of you. She wouldn't tell me why. She's the one who told me to look for you at Knickerbocker's. I think whatever dope scam you're involved in, she got out. I think she probably knew why Julie died, but she didn't want to talk about that either. Now she's dead, and you better have a good alibi for last night, 'cause if not, I'm going to give you up to a cop named Monaco out in Bayside so fast you won't even have time for your next costume change.''

"It's not dope, I told you."

"You're whining again. Skip on down. Where were you last night?''

"With Lettie."

"With Lettie. Lettie who's gone to London. Where with Lettie?''

"We went to a restaurant over on Lex, not too far from here. La Louisiana. Cajun food. You want to know what we had for dinner? I had gumbo, she had blackened redfish. Then we came back here.''

"And she left for London this morning."

"Right."

"Why a sudden trip to London?''

"School year's over, really. She's done with exams. We'd been planning this.''

"You smoke?''

"I ran out of Marlboros, but I've got some Camels, no filters. You want one?''

"I don't want one, but I need to smoke one." He opened up an old-fashioned cigarette box on the coffee table. The pack of Camels was inside. I shook one out and lit it, got through the first drag without choking.

"I think you're lying about the trip. I think the trip was planned suddenly, after somebody killed Sara Hildreth. I can tie this all into a package with Christmas wrapping paper if it's you.''

I don't know if it was the combination of Wild Turkey and Dos Equis and aspirin and Tylenol with codeine and Camel unfiltered, or just the mugging, but I was getting tired. When I get tired, my mind turns to pro wrestling announcer.

Scalia said, "You don't believe me about La Louisiana, go over there right now, ask the guy runs the place. I eat there all the time. I'm an excellent tipper.''

"I'm sure you are. But what time did you leave there?''

"Round midnight. I like to eat late."

"The cops figure Sara Hildreth was killed sometime between two and four in the morning. Still plenty of time for you to drop Lettie Schorr off at Weinstein, or the Hilton. By the way, what were you two doing at the Hilton that night?''

What night was it?

Scalia said, ''Lettie told me you followed us. Thought you were being slick.''

''That's me, slick. Repeat: What were you doing there?''

He jiggled the ice around in his drink, then sipped Glenlivet.

''Ahead of ourselves again.''

''Fine. You still had time to get out to Douglaston, kill her. The bartender at the place where she worked said she got a call early in the evening. It could have been you.''

''If she was so scared of me, why would she meet me?''

''I've been wondering about that myself.''

Scalia put his arms out. ''Because she didn't meet me. I know you don't think Lettie's so much of an alibi, but if she ever had to, she'd come back, tell the cops she was with me until six o'clock in the morning, when she went back over to Weinstein to finish packing for London.''

I finished the beer. ''Tell me again why you wanted to see me. I am fading fast.''

Scalia stood up, walked over to the picture window that looked down on Fifth Avenue, saw some dirt on the sill, wiped it away with his finger.

''I might want to go on camera with you.''

''Golly, Mike, there's good news.''

''You're still so fucking funny.'' He turned around, posing again, hands behind him, leaning on the windowsill. Bigtime college boy, telling me what the deal was. ''And so fucking smart? If you're so fucking smart, how come you haven't figured this out yet?''

I just watched him. It was his show now.

''I've saved up some money from my business dealings. But I need to get away for a while. Maybe a long while. Maybe never come back, that type of long while. So I'm going to need to put my hands on a little more money. I think you're going to want to give it to me.''

I reached into my wallet and pulled out a dollar bill.

"Here's a dollar, kid. Buy yourself a soda."

He let it go. He came back over, sat down.

"I've got a few things to work out with some, uh, associates of mine. But here's the way I want to structure this thing. Tomorrow, you come here with a crew about two in the afternoon. You bring me fifteen thousand dollars."

I stood up. "Forget it."

Scalia sat there, cool, like he was back at Knickerbocker's waiting for Lettie before I showed up and ruffled all his cock-pheasant feathers. "You bring me fifteen, I'll tell you everything you want to know."

"What makes you think the story is worth that kind of money?"

Scalia said, "Because it is."

"You're sure."

"Sure. I mean, it's an arbitrary number, fifteen thousand. But I think you're gonna think it's worth it. You talk to your people in the morning, work it out. Then call me. I'll be waiting for your call, and I'll be here at three."

"And if I don't?"

"Then I'll be gone, and you'll never know. And then you won't be as fucking smart as you like to think you are."

"What makes you think I won't come here with the money, do the interview, take the money back?"

Scalia stood up in his Polo sweatshirt and his tennis shorts and his high-white leather Reebok basketball sneakers, no socks.

"Because I got a feeling a deal's a deal with you. You think you're the good guys."

I had to admit, he had a point. I told him I would think it over and call him in the morning. Downstairs, I asked Valenzuela if he'd been working late the night before. He said it was my lucky day, he came on at midnight, went off at eight in the morning, he switched with the usual overnight man, Ray-Ray.

"You see Scalia and a tall blonde come in about the time you started your shift?"

Valenzuela still had the radio on. It sounded like Dolly Parton, but it could have been Loretta or Patsy. I knew less about female country singers than male country singers. Valenzuela scratched his head and said, "Sometimes, things happen so fass around here, I can' remember who is coming and going. You know?"

I took out a fifty. He looked at it like it had Estrella's picture on it.

"They come in about twel-thirty, she leave about sis-thirry."

I handed him the fifty. Suddenly, the whole world was a seller's market. The cabbie who picked me up out front of 24 Fifth didn't want to negotiate. He just flipped down the handle on the meter and took the good guys home.

CHAPTER

JEANNIE said, "You know what I was thinking yesterday? I was thinking I want to make love every day for the next month."

"Great. Put me down for two of them."

She was already sitting up in bed. I made a move in that direction, as a way of taking inventory. My knee usually sang the lead first thing in the morning. But now I had backup: sore back, sore hand from hitting Michael Scalia, sore cheek. Sore mouth. I made a moo sound.

"How do I look?"

She smiled brilliantly. She was wearing her blue nightgown, the long one. "Like Jake LaBamba."

I said, "LaMotta."

She put down the newspaper. Stroked my hair. "There's the boy. Do you want me to fix you breakfast in bed?"

I rubbed the last sleep out of my eyes, looked over at her.

"Breakfast in bed? Who are you? I'm calling the police."

"I'm being serious now. Can I get you something?"

"Make it the usual, in that case. Eggs over hard, English muffin, coffee, reconstructive surgery."

"Maybe we should just start with coffee. You want me to bring a straw?"

I swung my legs over the side of the bed and made a bigger moo sound than before. "Yes, darling," I said. "And here's what I'd like you to do with the straw."

Jeannie laughed and headed for the kitchen. "Now don't you be talking to the nurse that way, Mr. Raging Beast."

"Bull," I said.

IT was eight-thirty. We were in the living room having coffee and blueberry muffins Jeannie had heated up in the microwave. I was opposed to microwaves until we got one and I found out how quickly you could heat your muffins in the morning.

I caved in then on microwaves. Call forwarding would probably be next.

When I had gotten home from Scalia's, I had told Jeannie about everything except the two cigarettes.

"Would you pay him the money?" I said. I was in shirt, outside the jeans, and socks and sneakers. I had done some stretching exercises, showered, shaved over the bumps, dressed that far. Get that tie and blazer on me, look out, boys and girls, here comes Mr. Wizard.

"I've been thinking on that," Jeannie said. "I have, in fact, been thinking on the entire web of intrigue."

"Web of intrigue. I like that."

On the stereo, Elvis sang "Jailhouse Rock." Elvis was workout music for my wife. She was on the floor in sweats doing her own stretching exercises. They were part of a program named after a woman named Lotte Berk. I went to one Lotte Berk class with Jeannie. The class was in a Madison Avenue townhouse. It was a combination of yoga, aerobics, Marine boot camp, and a Lebanese prison. They taught various impossible pretzel things. Jeannie was doing one. She was sitting, back to me, right leg bent in front of her, foot pointing to her left, left leg bent behind her. She was holding on to the windowsill. She lifted the left leg about six inches off the ground and held it there.

She spoke without any strain in her voice, which I thought

was mildly interesting. "Anyway, I would pay the money.
First of all, whose money is it? Fay Zausner's money, right?
You know what fifteen thousand is to Fay Zausner? It's the
month of May in East Hampton. Or it's one quick pass
through Tiffany's. So don't worry about that. So what's left,
principles? I know you fancy yourself the home office there.
But checkbook journalism's been done before and been done
again, and just because *The Finley Report* doesn't have the
budget of *60 Minutes* doesn't mean it can't play by the same
rules. You're the best, sport. Top gun, you should pardon the
expression. You take more chances than those other shows.
A few too many to suit me, course, but you take them. You
do what you have to do, even if it means occasionally sacri-
ficing those, ahem, rugged good looks." Left leg down, deep
breath, left leg up. "So now you're running out of time, and
you're running out of people. This is your kind of piece:
something little that ends up looking real big. Where else do
you go if you don't play Scalia's game? You going to tie him
to his wet bar until he tells you the truth? I know you think
he's slicked you into a corner. Hell with that. You pays your
money, you takes your chances. Right?" She turned around,
smiled, shifted to left leg in front, right leg in back, deep
breath, lifted the right leg.

I ate some blueberry muffin, sipped some coffee. It was
not regulation coffee. It never is at the Finley apartment. She
said it was chocolate mocha decaffeinated, from Dean and
DeLuca's, designer deli on the West Side.

She figured she'd won with tobacco, caffeine was next,
even if there had been no formal announcement.

I said, "You think Charlie will go for it?"

"You think Charlie is going to pass up a chance for a) a
good story and b) a chance to goose the big Z?"

"Good point."

Jeannie said, "You think Scalia killed that girl?"

"I did. Now I'm not so sure. It's a good alibi, even if there
is a hole in it for Lettie Schorr. Ultimately, I guess I think if
he killed Sara Hildreth, he'd be in London with Lettie right
now, seeing the sights. My father always says that the cop's
worst nightmare is the alleged perpetrator who drops out of

nowhere, that you didn't even know existed. I think that might be the deal here. I think he's involved with Scalia and the dead ones, but I just haven't met him yet.''

Jeannie said, ''Or her.''

''Or her.''

''So play the hand you're dealt. Pay the money. Do the interview. Go from there.''

''You'd do it if it was a story for *Era*? One of your writers came to you, you'd say, Go?''

She was over on her back now, her body shaped like a little baby rocker, arms in the air, doing little stomach tighteners.

''I'd say, Go.'' She lay flat on the floor, took a deep breath, jumped up. She was showing off, we both knew it. She also was not sweating. ''Before you go, I want to give you something.'' She walked over to the kitchen counter, ripped off a piece of notepaper from the pad there, wrote something, folded it up, handed it to me. ''I told you I've been thinking on this. Don't look at that until after you get the poop from Michael Scalia. Then see if I'm right. 'Kay?''

I said okay, stuffed the note into the part of my wallet that still contained the key I'd found in Julie Samson's shoe box.

Then I went to work the telephone. I had to call Charlie Davidson, Marty Pearl, Captain Monaco, Gus Dancy.

And Michael Scalia, as the Beaver.

MARTY and I waited for Gus Dancy by the arch.

''You understand, the more we shoot here,'' Marty said, ''the more it gives continuity to the piece. Julie died over there. We talked to those two girls over there. We talk to the professor right here. You should have told me you were going back over to the room, incidentally, I would have gone with you. That would have been invigorating.'' He'd set the Betacam up on a tripod after checking a couple of different angles. ''Stand there for a second, don't move.''

I was directly underneath the arch, back to Fifth.

''Who knew someone would be following me? Who knew he'd double-team me? I'm still trying to figure out who the hell those guys are. They're not with Scalia.''

Marty said, "This shot will work peachy. Charlie really said okay on the money?"

"Not only did he say okay on the money, he wants to bring it in person, be there at Scalia's apartment when we do the interview."

"Field trip for the little guy, huh?"

I said, "His last words on the telephone were, and I quote, 'When old Fay finds out about this, I hope her tits unimplant.' Unquote. I guess it's possible. They reverse vasectomies, right?"

"And you talked to Scalia."

"I told him three o'clock, his place, certified check, if he was fucking around it was going to be round two."

"You're an animal, I mean it," Marty said. His red cap said, NABISCO GRAND PRIX. He said, "And from here we zip out to Douglaston?"

"Monaco said he would meet us at Sara Hildreth's at noon sharp. He said he shouldn't let me into the apartment, but there was something about me he just liked."

"I'm man enough to tell you the way the sun catches your bruises has always gotten me right here."

I looked at him. He was wearing the same sort of Polo sweatshirt Scalia had worn, only his was blue, with the sleeves rolled up. In my experience with Marty Pearl, it was the first time the little man on the horse had ridden across his bosom.

"You didn't buy that sweatshirt yourself. It was Mata Hari, wasn't it?"

"How do you do it?" Marty said. "How do you always know the right thing to say?"

I saw Gus Dancy walking across the park from the direction of Kornheiser, carrying coffee in an extra-large Styrofoam cup. He wore the usual uniform, but had added a paisley tie with the work shirt for the interview. His hair was brushed straight back. Maybe it had been sprayed a little.

"Gus Dancy," I said, "you're so vain, you prob'ly think this song is about you."

"Old Finley, I think of this as my television comeback. It is not like I've had to keep changing my phone number, people have been wanting to interview me so much on camera lately. I intend to be a small, albeit dashing, part of your piece." He nodded toward Marty. "This, I take it, is the estimable sidekick and artiste, Mr. Pearl."

Marty almost grinned. He said to me, "You're right, he can talk for a white man."

"Where do you want me?" Gus Dancy said, finishing the coffee and tossing it in a trash bin stuck behind the arch. Marty showed him. Gus said, "Tell me again why you need me? Are you getting close to a resolution?"

"Maybe," I said. Marty attached the mike to my tie, ran the wire down behind it, then down my pant leg. He did the same with Gus Dancy. "I just want you to talk some about Julie Samson the way you did in your office, then we'll vamp from there about what her side job might have been."

Marty said, "I'm rolling all the way." He stepped away from the camera, put the headphones on. "Sound checks from both of you please."

Gus said, "I have racked my brain and stretched my imagination since our dinner, but I have been unable to guess how she could have accumulated ten thousand dollars."

I said, "I'm hoping I'm going to find out today."

He looked at me. "Really?"

Marty got back behind the camera.

"Quiet on the set," he said. "Roll 'em."

Sometimes Marty just got silly in front of company.

"Professor Dancy," I began, "the late Julie Samson was a student of yours . . ."

Gus ran with it from there, like he was carrying the Olympic torch.

SARA Hildreth had lived upstairs in a yellow two-story Cape with flaking paint and black shutters and a fence on both sides of the front walk and a toy yard on both sides of the fence that looked like it belonged in an old black-and-white sitcom. The house was about a hundred yards from the Douglaston stop on the Long Island Railroad, and Monaco said it was owned by a Mrs. Sullivan. Monaco met us out in front of the house. Mrs. Sullivan, arms folded, watched us from one of her windows.

Monaco nodded toward the window as he led us up the walk. "You probably want to interview Mrs. Sullivan. She's got a very bubbly, winning personality. Has a lot of valuable insights on the youth of America. Talks about the moral decay of the country like it's tooth decay."

I said, "I'll bet she does. She have any solutions?"

"Yeah. More bran."

There was an outside stairway on the side of the house that led upstairs. Monaco led the way again. He was wearing a blue suit and a white shirt. I noticed the back of the collar was fraying. Jeannie said that was very aristocratic. She told me why once, but I'd forgotten.

I said to Monaco, "Do you know why frayed shirt collars are supposed to be aristocratic?"

Monaco stopped before he opened the door, looked at me. He probably didn't mean it, but there was some fun in the eyes. "You're the type always was busting his old man's balls, asking where the fucking wind came from, right?"

"Ah-hah," I said. "You don't know either."

We went inside. Inside was still a mess. Couch cushions behind the couch, desk drawers pulled out, emptied on top of the desk, on the floor, books from the living room's one bookcase all over the floor. We went into the small bedroom. Same in there. Mattress on the floor, clothes in a pile, shoes out of shoe boxes. Rug pulled up.

Monaco said, "I don't think it was pro, but it seems to have been fairly thorough." He ran an impatient hand through his curly hair. He did that a lot. "You got any idea what they mighta been looking for here?"

From the living room, Marty called, "Okay if I shoot?"

Monaco said, "Why not?"

I said, "As a matter of fact, I don't know what whoever it was was looking for. We're assuming this happened after she died?"

"It would be a safe assumption."

"And I'm assuming Mrs. Sullivan didn't see or hear anything."

"Fast asleep. Said that since Mr. Sullivan died, Lord rest his soul they had forty-two wonderful years together, she can't even stay awake past *Knots Landing* anymore. Didn't know anything was amiss until we came by in the morning."

"So Sara Hildreth had a date with somebody. Met him at Arleigh Beach. He killed her. There?"

"There," Monaco said. "Water in the water was same as water in the lungs. There was also some skin under her fingernails, probably belonging to the one who did it. And I got a footprint from the beach area that matches a print down by the steps here."

I said, "He came back here looking for something, which he may or may not have found."

Monaco leaned against the bedroom window, stuffed his hands in his pockets. "You want to tell me what this is all about?"

"Captain, I wish I knew what this is all about. I got beat up last night by two guys who shouldn't have any relation to anything that I can see, except trying to scare me and my people off."

"I wish I had people I could call my people."

"You know what I mean."

"Guys came in, dusted. They actually got a few partials might be able to help us out, we ever get a suspect that is. You got a suspect, Mr. Finley?"

He looked at me with what my father used to call "white lights." No more fun in them now. They were the eyes for the room at the station where you took the baddies and asked them the questions. "It wasn't considered good form to beat confessions out of them with your fists, sonny," my dad said once. "So you tried to do it with eyes white as the light they were sitting under. White lights. Make 'em full of threat as you could." Monaco tried. I smiled. Thought about Scalia.

No reason for him to be in America if he'd killed Sara Hildreth.

No reason for him to call me. Fifteen thousand dollars wasn't enough to pay for the extra day or two that might cost you a murder rap.

"Captain," I said. "A linear thinker like me, I understand

homicide investigations. If I had a suspect, I'd tell you. Sara Hildreth didn't tell me why she left school suddenly. She borrowed three thousand dollars from Julie Samson a while ago. Mr. Arthur Samson told me that. I don't know why. I think Sara Hildreth and Julie Samson were involved in some tricky sort of dope scam, but I don't have any evidence other than some big cash I found in Julie Samson's room at Washington Square University. I think there is a chance they might be bit players in some bigger production, but for the life of me, I can't get a handle on it. Do I think there is a connection between the two deaths? Yeah, I do. Now we both do. Now I feel like I've had this conversation with everyone except Mrs. Sullivan downstairs.'' I bent down, put a pair of small pink running shoes with the white Nike swoosh into a Nike box. Sara Hildreth's pink running shoes. Couldn't have been more than a girl's size six. Sad little girl's shoes. ''Am I getting pissed off? Uh huh. Usually by now, I'm the leader in the clubhouse, the other players are trying to catch me, and I'm at the nineteenth hole having a drink.''

Monaco came off the windowsill, opened the window, took a new cigar out of his inside pocket, bit off the end, spit the end out the window. He lit the cigar. He was as gentle with them as Marty was; it was as if they were smoking snakes.

''So what are we looking for here?''

''Checkbook?''

Monaco said, ''Nope. And no little money ledger, and no address book and no little book with phone numbers in it. Aren't all those things standard issue with women?''

''Maybe the perp took them because there was stuff about him in them.''

''You want to look around some more?''

I had heard Marty go clumping down the steps. Now I heard him come back up. ''I don't think so. I'm getting a little tired going through dead girls' things. You think you'll turn up anything with the prints?''

Monaco was squatting near the nightstand, looking at a pad of paper. ''Not unless whoever did it has been a bad boy some other time in his life.'' He stuffed the pad in the pocket of his jacket.

Downstairs, Monaco said, ''Call me. Anything you get. Call me.''

I told him I would call him. ''You want to watch me do a stand-up?''

Monaco opened the door to his car, and stood there, like he was thinking about it. ''Call me,'' he said. He made an illegal U-turn and headed back toward Northern Boulevard. I did the stand-up with Mrs. Sullivan's yellow Cape in the background.

It was when we were in the van on the Cross Island heading back to Manhattan that Marty pulled up his blue Polo sweatshirt and took the white envelope from where he'd stuffed it in his pants for safekeeping.

Marty said, ''Mail came while you were in the bedroom with Monaco. I saved Mrs. Sullivan a trip. She gave me a cruller.''

Sara Hildreth's phone bill.

Marty said, ''You never know.''

I said, ''How do you do it? How do you always know the right thing to say?''

CHAPTER
22

TWO o'clock. We were waiting for Charlie Davidson in front of the Crazy Eddie's on West Fifty-seventh. Crazy Eddie's was on the ground floor. Channel A's studios were on six. Charlie said he'd meet us out front with the money, and we'd go down to Scalia's apartment together.

"The sound isn't perfect," Marty was saying. "But when we're shooting on the run like we do, you don't need perfect sound. Mostly, it just saves wear and tear on me. I don't mind doing pictures and sound. Really don't. It makes me feel like I've got hands on all the time, but I get tired of lugging the mini, plus the damn recorder in that Porta Brace knapsack, plus the tripod when we need it. The Porta Brace gets to feel like a frigging Snuggli after a while. I either go to this new combination deal, or I hire a sherpa."

He was happy as he gets, talking about television hardware, while we waited to go see Scalia. I was just there.

"It just streamlines the whole thing, building the sound stuff right into the camera," he said.

The van was facing west, toward the Hudson. There had been some talk that Fay Zausner was going to move Channel A out from above the video store and off West Fifty-seventh, and over to New Jersey somewhere. No one knew where. Secaucus? Hackensack?

I said, "I don't want to move to New Jersey."

"Nobody does, unless they're a gas station. Are you listening?"

"My mind was wandering."

"Gee, there's a surprise announcement."

"You told me to stop thinking about what Scalia might tell us. You said stop thinking about the whole thing, that we should just let it happen."

"Exactly. Where was I?" He pushed the red Nabisco cap back, and showed some of his thick red hair. "Oh. Anyway, they call it a Camcorder, that's the nickname for when it's all one piece. You don't even have to hook up headsets to it if you don't want to. There's a speaker, comes right out the back. You hear what you're recording like it was the playback on a tape recorder."

I said, "Oh?"

"Yeah. I was thinking today, I don't know why, but you know how long I've had those Beyers?"

"Beyers?"

"The headsets. I think it's going on five years."

I tilted my head at him, gave him a look that said, Is that so? Five years? I looked at the door Charlie would be coming out of and wondered where the hell the little guy was.

"Marty, don't take this in a negative way, but is this a situation like where now you're talking and you're never going to stop?"

"Thank you very much," Marty said. "I'm trying to pass the time in an informative way. Basically, I'm just thinking Sony might not even be the way to go anymore. Some of the guys at Channel Two and Channel Four have gone to this new Ikegami HL-95, the Something-Cam. Ultra-Cam, Uni-Cam, Cam-Cam. I forget. But you can record to a Sony Beta deck off it. It's supposed to be the new hot number, a little more prestigious than the Betacam. I've got to ask Charlie about it when he gets here."

"When he gets here. Ikegami, you said?"

The little guy came out, jockey size, in his favorite seersucker suit, about two-fifteen. I got into the back seat, he jumped into the front next to Marty.

"Good afternoon, boys, sorry about the delay."

I said, "You have the money?"

Charlie turned around, pulled the bank check out of his inside pocket, showed it to me. Fifteen thousand dollars. Mr. Michael Scalia.

"Your boss like the idea?"

"I hope she will," Charlie said. "Vanna left for Switzerland this morning." Marty pulled onto Eleventh Avenue, which meant he was going to take the West Side Highway.

I said, "What are you saying?"

Charlie smiled, innocent as a cherub. "What am I saying? Other than we're probably talking careers on the line here?"

Marty said, "You didn't ask her if you could spend fifteen and then three zeroes dollars for an interview that we don't know what's in it exactly?"

Charlie said, "Fuck Vanna, okay, boys?"

LEA was waiting for us in the lobby at 24 Fifth. The concierge who looked like St. Nick, McKelvy, was back behind the desk. I gave him my name, he told us Mr. Scalia was expecting us. Marty carried the camera and the Porta Brace. I carried the lights and the tripod. Charlie carried the check. We all got into the elevator.

"When I was at Loyola University," Charlie said, "the old frat house didn't look anything like this. How does he get to class, by limo?"

I said, "Only if school weren't so close."

Marty said to Lea, "You're sure that recorder works through your sweatshirt."

She was wearing a baggy white sweatshirt with NIKE written diagonally in oversized blue letters across the front. Underneath was the best hand-sized tape recorder Channel A could provide. She was wearing it in a harness she'd rigged herself, and fastened somehow to her bra. She'd offered to show it to us while we waited for the elevator, but Charlie ahemmed and said, "We trust that it's ingenious, dear."

Lea smiled. "I've been practicing it all morning with Martha Bryne. From across the hall. The sound is fine, even if I move around some. And I don't have to be as close to him as you think.''

Marty said, "Tell me again how much time to a side."

Lea said, "One hour."

"Then you make sure you keep an eye on your watch. I don't want to be changing *my* tape, and all of a sudden nobody's talking and he hears your breasts make a sound like they're shutting off. When you get close to an hour, you excuse yourself and say you have to go to the little girls' room.''

She nodded. To me she said, "Why do we need this again?''

"I'll field that one," Charlie said. "There is no need for us to trouble Mr. Scalia with this, but for fifteen thousand dollars in a guaranteed contract like the ballplayers get, nothing here today is going to be completely off the record. We are going to fudge a little bit, even if he drops a pearl when Marty is changing those tapes.''

Lea said, "Is this good journalism?''

I said, "No, but it's excellent business.''

The elevator doors opened. We all got out. Marty said, "Start the tape, darlin'.''

SCALIA had done everything except go to makeup. He wore a summer suit of a color somewhere between gray and blue with a faint pinstriped pattern to it and a white buttoned-down shirt and a yellow power tie with what looked like teardrops all over it. His hair was so moussed up I thought if Marty looked down, he could see his reflection in it.

I wondered idly if Michael Scalia had done his nails.

Lea whispered, "Suit by Perry Ellis. Five hundred if it's a dime. Hair by *Tango Argentina*.''

Scalia didn't offer his hand. Neither did any of us. He looked at Charlie and said, "Who's this?''

Charlie was perfect. Gave it three beats, looked Scalia over like he was a pony Charlie was thinking of buying for his grandchildren. I was waiting for him to walk over and pull Scalia's lips back, look at his teeth, when he sighed and said to me, "He is exactly as you described him." He looked at Scalia again. "I am Charlie Davidson, son. I run Channel A. I'm the one with the money."

"Can I see it, please?" Scalia said.

We were still in the foyer. Marty and Lea had moved around us and Marty was doing setting-up things in the middle of the living room with the tripod and a couple of chairs Lea had brought from the kitchen.

Charlie took the check out of his suit and held it up in front of Scalia, who reached for it, as Charlie wanted, just as Charlie pulled it out of his reach. Charlie smiled at the college boy in the expensive suit grabbing for the money, nearly stumbling into me when Charlie put it behind his back.

"Not so fast, son."

Scalia flushed. He looked at me. It was the same hard look he'd tried at Knickerbocker's. It still needed work.

"You want to play games? You want to play games, try getting your story out of Julie or Sara."

I took a half-step closer to him. "Have you forgotten last night so quickly? Don't speak harshly to me, Michael."

Charlie said. "Easy does it, both of you. We are here to conduct business. Our business, your business. I am going to hand over this check to you, and we are going to do the interview. Once I hand you the check, the money is yours. The lads will not take it back from you." He grinned. "Which they could." He held the check far out in front of him with both hands, like he was trying to read it without his reading glasses. "And the station will not stop payment on it. But this is a lot of money. We have paid for interviews before when I thought the occasion merited it. But never quite this much. So before we begin, you tell me just what it is you were involved in, with Julie Samson and the other dead girl, Miss Hildreth. You tell me right now."

Scalia looked at the check, then Charlie, then me.

"Is he telling the truth?"

I said, "It's what he does. He tries to lie, he cramps up."

Scalia said, "Julia Samson and Sara Hildreth were two of my girls, okay?"

I said, "Two of your girls?"

Scalia sighed. "You haven't gotten it all along, have you, man? You came down here with all your own college ideas, all full of it about the days when you had your fist up in the air in the park, smoking a joint, trying to change the world. You probably have been walking around with tears in your eyes, thinking about the good old days at old Washington Square U." He shook his head at me, disgusted. "Julie Samson and Sara Hildreth were part of my escort service, man. I ran it right out of The Square."

Lea Ballard had come over to stand next to us, holding the headset in her hand.

I said, "They were prostitutes?"

"Well, sonofabitch," Michael Scalia said, reaching over and taking the check from Charlie this time. "You've gone and cracked the fucking case."

SCALIA and I sat facing each other. Marty was set up behind me, shooting Scalia, tight as he could I was sure, over my shoulder. Lea was next to Marty, kneeling, headsets on. Marty had checked the sound himself, just told her to put up a hand if a siren went by on the street, or a bomb went off, we'd stop. Charlie sat on the couch with a notebook, writing down my questions in case we wanted to do reverses when the interview was over. Scalia had a glass of water near his skinny, buffed, black wingtip shoes.

I had told him to start the way he wanted, as long as we finished with Julie Samson.

"I had a friend from, you know, my old neighborhood who had started up one of these escort services a few years ago," Scalia was saying. "This was before the Mayflower Madam, any of that. He ran it out of an office just like a legitimate, I don't know, secretarial service. Business cards. Ads in the Yellow Pages. Ads in *New York* magazine and the *Village Voice*, like that. And good-looking young women who looked about as far from streetwalkers as you could get. You understand? I could see the deal was to make the whole deal as antihooker as possible. Like, oh, I'm paying for this?"

Scalia did some summer work for his friend. If it was an out-of-town call, Connecticut or Long Island or New Jersey, he would drive the women, pick them up. He helped out on the phones sometimes. He even helped his friend recruit at bars and restaurants and discos and even casting calls for actresses.

I said, "And you never had any trouble finding enough women to act essentially as prostitutes."

"Let me tell you something. First, not all the pretty women in New York City are on the cover of *Elle*, or starring in *Phantom of the Opera*, maybe you've noticed. Second, there are an awful lot of them just barely surviving, you know, out there. I offered them a chance to make some money, not wait tables."

"So you finally decided to go into business for yourself."

"Sure."

"And you decided to use women from Washington Square University. Why is that exactly?"

"I paid attention when I worked for my friend, kept my eyes open, listened to everything he said, saw how he pushed all the buttons. And one thing stood out, for me at least. He, my friend, said the most callbacks he got, you know, repeaters, were for the younger-looking ones. My friend always told me you couldn't have enough prom queens. That's what college is, right? A convention of prom queens."

My side was starting to hurt. I shifted a little to my right, but made sure not to get in Marty's shot. "Can I ask you something?" I said. "Why were you in college in the first place?"

"I wanted to see if anything straight was ever going to appeal to me. If there was some straight way of going at things I didn't know about, coming from where I came from."

"The alternative was finding something with a friend from the neighborhood?"

"Basically. Then, as I was saying, I decided I could do both."

"How did you start?"

"My friend had gotten out of the business by then, and he promised to help me out with old client lists. Ultimately, a business like this is run through referrals and word of mouth. You're always gonna do more there than with the ads. I couldn't do television commercials with satisfied customers. Then I got a partner."

"Why did you need a partner?"

Scalia smiled for the camera. "If I had the kind of money I wanted, I wouldn't have needed to go into business in the first place. Being a struggling college student"—he made a move like he was fixing his tie knot, even though it didn't need fixing—"never appealed to me."

"Your partner was also from The Square?"

"Man, you're still going real slow, aren't you? My partner was Sara Hildreth. I didn't know Julie yet, but I knew Sara from, you know, around school. We took a couple of classes together. She acted as a middleman a couple of times, helped me buy a couple of grades, for a percentage. So I could tell right off she liked money the way I liked money. I figured as much as I thought I knew about the business end of it, and as much as I thought I knew about women, I still needed a woman. The Mayflower Madam's situation doesn't run the same way without her being a woman, I don't think. That's just my opinion. Anyway, Sara borrowed three thousand dollars from Julie, enough to make the security deposit and first-month rent on a cheap apartment downtown we could use as an office."

"What did she tell Julie, to get that kind of money?"

"You know, I don't even remember. But Sara wanted something, she got it."

"Why didn't you tell me about Sara before?"

"You weren't paying me before."

I said, "What a guy."

He and Sara advertised in the school paper, *The Square Deal*. Said the tone of it was, "College students, do you want a head start in the high-powered world of New York City public relations? Salaries up to $500 a week!" That sort of thing. Called the company Extra Credits. Scalia put a phone number with the ad. The women who called, he interviewed himself, told them what the real business was. The male students from The Square, he told all the public relations positions had been filled.

"I laid it out for them," he said. "I told them they were being paid for their *time*, not sex, and if sex was involved, it would be by their choice. I told them we were starting out at a hundred dollars an hour, five hundred for the night, any tips they got, and the tips would probably be for sex, they could keep. We just took a percentage of the flat rate. Fifty percent for them, fifty percent came right back to Extra Credits. I told them at the start, almost all of the work would be at night, we'd take it from there later on, see if they wanted to do weekends. Even matinees during the week."

Extra Credits had officially opened the fall of the previous school year. He started out with four coeds from The Square, two airline flight attendants who worked part time, two high school seniors, two secretaries to work the phones. Scalia and Sara ran the business, handling the scheduling and the appointments themselves, keeping the books. When business began to pick up, some of the escorts would occasionally help out on the phone.

I said, "You recruited high school seniors?"

Scalia said, "You ever been up Second Avenue on a Friday night? It's all they are, high school girls looking to score cocaine and party and meet older guys. Show how grown-up they are. Most of 'em can afford their own dope, but not all of them."

"Was one of the original four Julie Samson?"

"No, but Sara Hildreth was."

"She ran the business and hooked too?"

"I told you. She liked money. I don't know what her old man did before he died, but she used to talk so much about never being hungry again, she sounded like fucking Scarlett O'Hara." He put his hands out. "This is cable, right? I can say fuck?"

"You're perfect. I mean it."

Scalia said, "The funny thing about Sara was, she was gay, she said the sex part didn't mean much to her, one way or another. She said it would have been like stealing if she only had to have sex, it was listening to the old farts all night that was the hard part.''

"Why did she get out?"

He looked sideways, like he was deciding something.

"We started fighting about everything. What girls should go with what clients. What they should wear. Whether we should raise the rates to two hundred an hour, for chrissakes. Everything. Sara thought threesomes were okay, I didn't like it for the image I wanted Extra Credits to give off. I finally told her she was out.''

"Just like that? You said you were partners.''

"It wasn't like we'd signed a prenuptial agreement when we went into business. I gave her back her original three thousand, gave her three on top of it, and told her to get lost.''

"She went for that?''

"Fuck no. She said she was going to call the cops, close me down, put ads next to my ads, telling people what I was doing. I told her I'd kill her.''

"You were prepared to kill her?''

He tried to look wounded.

"What do you take me for? I wasn't gonna kill anybody. All I was interested in was making her think I would do it. I started to bounce her around one night, told her there was nowhere she could go I wouldn't find her.''

"And she left school after that?''

"She left school.''

"Who killed her?''

"You know what I think? I think Sara tried to go into business for herself out there in Douglaston, and she just picked the wrong guy, he got rough with her and killed her accidentally.''

I said, "Back up: Lettie Schorr was one of the original four from school?''

Scalia put up a hand. "You can stop that thing, right?'' I turned around to Marty. "It's okay,'' I said. Marty backed away from the tripod and stretched. Lea took off the headsets, stood up, stretched herself. Charlie just stared at Scalia. Scalia leaned forward. "Listen, she was, but I'm not going to say that on camera. I'm gonna say it about Julie because she's dead. I said it about Sara because she's dead. You check out my alibi on her, by the way?'' I told him Valenzuela backed up his story. He said, ''But there's no need to put Lettie's name on television. Lettie's always, you know, done it to buy dope. And now she's out and I'm out, so I'm just going to say no about her.'' I said, forget it, we wouldn't even use the question.

I looked at Lea. She nodded. If I ever needed Lettie Schorr for anything, I had Lea's tape as a bargaining chip.

I said, ''Let's go.''

Marty and Lea got back into position. Marty checked the shot. Lea handed him the headsets. ''Wait till we have speed,'' Marty said. I turned around. He made a firing motion at me with his index finger, handed the headsets back to Lea.

Scalia backed up and talked more about the business. He was Rockefeller talking about Standard Oil. The women of Extra Credits were to dress a certain way. The flat fee was to be paid up front, the tips later. Slowly he built on the client list his friend had staked him to. Scalia said there were all kinds of clients, businessmen from New York, from out of town, rich Arabs, visiting athletes, a few politicians, a television evangelist. The phones were shut down after one in the morning, he said, to eliminate the drug calls. The price for an hour went up fifty dollars an hour, seven hundred for the night.

''We supplied them with an illusion of virgins, to tell you the truth,'' Scalia said. ''And they were willing to pay top dollar for that.''

I asked him about the television evangelist.

''It wouldn't have been the Reverend Eugene Endicott of the World Christian Network,'' I said, and heard Charlie snort, remembering the phony preacher Channel A and I had made into the first Jim Bakker a few years before.

Scalia said it wasn't Endicott.

I thought, shit, it would have been fun to dress Endicott up in one more bonnet.

If it was a new client, Scalia would deliver Sara or Lettie or one of the flight attendants or one of the high school girls himself, show himself when he dropped them at a hotel usually. He even started carrying a handgun, he said, just in case, even though he never had to use it.

I said, "It was the gun Julie Samson shot herself with."

Scalia said, "That was my fault. Not her, you know, killing herself. I think she was gonna do that anyway. She would've found a way. But the day before she did it, she came over to my apartment and told me she wanted to talk. I left the room, and she must've taken it then. I was closing the business down by then. She had started seeing someone, nobody knew who it was, and she said it wasn't going well, she needed someone to talk to. With Sara gone, I was her only friend."

"Back up again. Why were you closing the business down?"

"Man, it wasn't the cops who finally got me. They got close but you could pay 'em off. No. It was the goddamned surgeon general. The whole time we were starting the business, nobody worried about diseases or anything, we figured we were getting a high-class clientele and so forth. I know it sounds dumb, but it's the way they all thought. It can't happen to me. But AIDS was different, man. Even at the start, they didn't seem to pay it much attention. Finally, though, it seemed like every day, there was a new scare or something in the papers or on television. I told 'em they were worried, get tested. They did. None of 'em had it. But all I started to hear about from them was high risk."

I said, "Imagine that."

"Yeah. Anyway, a couple quit. Then a couple more. We had about twenty girls working then. Finally, I was down to ten, then eight. They'd use different reasons, but I knew what the bottom line was. AIDS. Julie and Lettie were two of the final eight. Sara was out of the picture."

"Were Julie and Lettie proud to be quarterfinalists?"

"Huh?"

"Forget it. Go on."

"Well, Mike Scalia didn't have to be hit over the head with a ballpeen hammer. It was over. When you followed me to the Hilton the other night, it was Lettie's last call. This

Kuwaiti guy, liked to pay her the five hundred, tip her a thousand. I went over with him, not because I was worried about him, just to thank him for his business, tell him this was it. He tipped her two grand, and Extra Credits was out of business. Officially. Close the books.''

I took a sip of water. Looked over at Charlie. ''You mind that this is all over the place?''

He shook his head. ''It's called conversation. You're perfect.''

''Back up again then,'' I said to Scalia. ''How did you get Julie involved in the first place?''

''I didn't, actually. Sara did. They were roommates, remember. It didn't take long for Julie to figure out what Sara was doing. I met her through Sara. She said she wanted to do it. I said to her, 'You've got a rich daddy, why do you want to do it?' She said, 'Because of my rich daddy.' ''

''What did that mean? She hate her father?''

''Oh, man. I don't mean to sound disrespectful of the dead . . .''

''Not you, Mike.''

''. . . but the only time she ever got real passionate was when she got talking about how much she hated her old man.''

''She ever say why?''

''One night when she was drunk. She went off on this tirade about how it had taken her her whole life, something like that, how it was his turn, the no-good so-and-so. See how he liked it for a change. I couldn't make heads or tails of it, she was so goddamned mad. But when I asked her about it in the morning, she clammed up.''

''The mugging in February Lea told me about, that was a client who beat Julia up, wasn't it?''

''A Colombian. We knew he was in the cocaine business, but we thought he was, you know, a gentleman. She was lucky to get out of there. It'd been somebody else, from a different line, I would have sent somebody over to talk with him. But not a Colombian. Not from that line.''

''You eventually had an affair with Julie.''

Scalia said, ''Yes.''

"You had an affair with her, even though she was working for you."

The minute I asked the question, I thought, Right, Finley, they were operating under the same rules as the Chase Manhattan. No office fraternization.

Scalia said, "I went out with a lot of my girls," then did the business with the tie knot again.

I said, "Pimps do that, right?"

Scalia's hand stayed where it was, like it was his new tie clasp. "What did you call me?"

"Pimp."

He had enjoyed it up to now, a clever young businessman on the go, dressed smart, shooting the interview right here in the smart apartment, fifteen grand in his pocket, bags probably packed for Europe, using the same tone of voice to talk about live girls, dead girls, high school girls.

Scalia said, "I'm not going to sit here and let you call me a pimp on television."

I said, "Until I've run out of tape, I would like to see you leave."

This time he didn't tell Marty to stop tape. So it was all going to look prettier than a spread in *House and Garden* on the air. Scalia turned to Charlie and said, "Can he call me a pimp?"

Charlie said, "Son, you call Lassie a dog, right?"

We were still rolling.

Scalia said, "I didn't think of myself as a pimp."

"I know, you thought of yourself as an investment banker from Goldman, Sachs. Was it you seeing some of the other young women from Extra Credits that caused your relationship with Julie Samson to end? You told me once before that it was you who broke it off."

Scalia looked at me warily now. When he spoke some of the car-phone strut had gone out of his voice. "It was funny. What she was doing, you know, with the company, she didn't see as a problem with us seeing each other. But me being with another girl, *that* was a problem. So I told her we had to break it off if she wanted to keep working."

He went to the tie again. He was starting to remind me of

a third base coach. Take or swing away? I noticed there was some makeup on his upper lip, where I'd hit him.

"She agreed?"

"Yeah, and I've got to admit, I was relieved, man. She was *suffocating*, Julie. She tried to suffocate me. I figure she was trying to suffocate the new guy, whoever he was. I'm no psychologist, but maybe it had something to do with the fact that she hated her old man like she did. Even though she knew we were closing down, she started to get like hysterical at the end. She was afraid that when we closed down Extra Credits, she was gonna be alone, or something. Plus, she always talked about needing money."

"For what?"

"She never said."

"Did you know she had ten thousand dollars in her room?"

"I didn't know how much until you told me. I figured she had something, the way she always talked."

"But why?"

"I'm telling you, man. I don't know."

"Why'd she kill herself, Scalia?"

"I don't know!" He yelled it. The yelling didn't go with the Perry Ellis. "Guilt, maybe. I don't *know*! She was fucking unstable. I'm sorry. Maybe she'd gone around the bend. Maybe her new boyfriend would know, if you could find him. Maybe she made up the new boyfriend, trying to make me jealous."

"You sure you don't know who the boyfriend was?"

"No. Shit, maybe it was one of the clients. That had happened before. A little wine, a little candlelight, big tip, they think they're in love."

"You have your client list?"

"It's gone. I burned it. Sara took her copy with her when she left."

"You're lying."

"Swear. You want a client list, get hers. It could be in her apartment, far as I know. Or she burned hers. Or threw it in the Sound. I don't give a shit."

I said, "We're paying you a lot of money for this interview."

Scalia said, "I don't care if you invite me over to your house at Christmas and let me play Santa Claus. If I still had it, I wouldn't give it up. I dealt with those people in good faith."

From where he sat, Charlie said, "Don't forget Jeannie."

I said, "Can you think of anyone who might have had a reason to try to scare me off this story?"

"As a matter of fact, it's the part I can't figure. Unless, like I said, it was this client boyfriend of Julie's, afraid you were going to find out who he was. I asked around, trying to help out, you know, tried to call some friends. I came up empty."

I said, "What a guy."

Scalia said, "We're done here?"

We weren't quite done. In television, you are rarely done. It is somewhat like tennis without tie breakers that way.

Marty told Scalia to stay where he was for a minute, and moved the tripod behind him. Marty said, "And don't move your head or your hands all the time like you did when the camera was on you." Charlie read me back five or six questions, I asked them again. Scalia started to get up again, Marty told him to stay put and talk to me. Scalia said he and Lettie were thinking about going to the south of France. Had I ever been to one of those nude beaches at St. Tropez, or anyplace?

I nodded and frowned for Marty.

Finally Marty said, "Done."

I said to Scalia, "Write down the names of as many of your escorts as you can, and whether they were students or stewardesses or high school girls, and phone numbers."

"Forget it. Why should I give them up either?"

"Because we paid you all that money. Because I'm not going on the air with the word of college-boy pimp without somebody to verify it. One way or another, we're going to get one of your debutantes to go on camera, even if we have to threaten to tell daddy on her. Because if you don't give me names, I call a Detective Monaco at the One-hundred-eleventh in Bayside and tell him you were running a call girl ring with

Sara Hildreth, and we'll see how he likes your alibi, and what he thinks when he hears you're going to get to St. Tropez."

Marty reached into the pocket of his painter's pants. "I think I've got a felt-tip in here somewhere," he said.

Scalia said, very funny, and sat down at his desk, and wrote. He said no phone numbers, just names. The phone numbers had been in the Extra Credits books.

I said, "Put little stars next to the names of the high school girls. You can leave out who their favorite living Americans are."

When he was done, I took the list. There were fifteen names on it. I didn't recognize any of them, but there was no reason why I should have. Maybe Lea would later. Or Gus Dancy.

Scalia said, "Now we're done?"

"We're done," I said.

Charlie opened the front door and said, "It's been an honor." Marty and Lea went first, then Charlie. I was last with the Porta Brace. Scalia started to close the door. I stopped it with the Porta Brace, made a neat little pivot, and hit him a straight left hand.

I was pretty sure that this time I broke Michael Scalia's fucking nose.

WHEN we got downstairs, I asked St. Nick if I could borrow his phone, got information, dialed the number, said to the woman who answered, "Detective Monaco, please." Monaco was in the office. I told him what I knew about Michael Scalia. I told him he better get into town, because I didn't know when Scalia was leaving for Europe.

"Hey," Monaco said. "Thanks."

"Get a grip on yourself, man. Don't go all to pieces with gratitude. I'm just doing what any good citizen would do." Monaco didn't laugh. He just hung up the phone.

I hung up Valenzuela's house phone, turned to the group. "Now we're done," I said.

CHAPTER
24

I SAID, "Is that bracelet African, Desmond?"

He said, "Tiffany's, actually."

Marty had gone home. Lea had gone off to an AA meeting. Charlie had gone back to the office. I was standing in Desmond Akeem Powell's tiny office at Kornheiser. I had walked in without knocking. The shirt was all white today, suspenders yellow, tie a yellow print. Earring still in place. The silver bracelet.

I said, "Michael Scalia just told me Sara Hildreth brokered grades. A couple of years ago, you got accused of selling a grade. Was Sara Hildreth involved?"

"She was not involved. I did not even know her then. This is the truth, I swear to you."

"It is kind of unusual, don't you think? You were Julie's friend. She was Julie's roommate. She helped in the buying and selling of grades. You got accused of selling a grade."

He put the big hands palm down on his desk. Used them to keep him in his seat. "And was cleared of those charges, sir. Of charges made by an unstable young woman named Montgomery, Jessie Montgomery, Jessica Montgomery, who graduated from this fine school and ended up almost imme-

diately in an institution, because of a nervous breakdown. If
you would like to confirm that for yourself, feel free. It is the
truth.''

"How come you haven't called me, Desmond? I've been
calling you. You don't like me?''

"I was at Stanford, for my reunion. My tenth, Mr. Finley.
I found all your messages waiting for me last night. I was
going to call you today.''

There were photographs all over the walls of the dark office. Elephants and lions. An African sunset. Monkey in a
tree. They were of professional quality, mounted the same
way.

"Yours?'' I said, pointing to the largest one. It showed a
lion sleeping in the golden grass Jeannie had described.

"Yes. Photography is a hobby.''

"You told me you didn't like Sara Hildreth.''

He sighed, and leaned back in his chair. I heard music
coming from a radio somewhere, or an unseen stereo. It was
George Benson. "I did not lie. I did not like Sara Hildreth.
The little I knew of her, I could see she bullied Julie. Julie
said she was always loaning her money. If she had tried to
get me to sell a grade, I wouldn't have liked her. She did not
try to get me to sell a grade. I still did not like her. I tell you
the truth.''

"Sara Hildreth is dead, did you know that?''

The flawless skin pulled back from the eyes. He swallowed. Took a breath. Exhaled through his mouth. If it wasn't
real shock, it was pretty good.

"How?''

"Murdered in Douglaston, where she was living and
working. Drowned in an area known as Arleigh Beach.''

He twisted the silver bracelet around on his wrist. "You
think it is somehow connected with Julie?''

"I don't know. I think so. I thought I knew just about
everything until Scalia talked about the grades. I came here
to see if there was a connection between you and Sara Hildreth.''

Desmond Akeem Powell said, "Sir, I have not seen her
in months. I was in California when she died. I have no

reason to lie to you. I will not mourn Sara, but I have nothing to do with her death.''

''They were involved in a prostitution ring, I just found that out,'' I said. ''Scalia and Julie and Sara. Others. I thought you should know before I went on the air with it.''

The move was quick as one of the cats in his pictures, Desmond Akeem Powell coming across the desk with long arms and strong hands and grabbing the front of Peter Finley, who was still standing up.

''You are a liar.'' He had shirt, blazer, me. He made it seem easy. Even leaning over the desk, he was a head taller. I was getting a much better look at the earring. His breath was coming in big, loud gulps. I said, ''It's the truth. Scalia told me. He had no reason to lie. Now I'm telling you the truth, Desmond. So let go.'' He held on another fifteen seconds, pushed me back and let go, pulled back across the desk, took more deep breaths, staring at me with big eyes, the whites looking beyond white set against his skin. ''You tell me,'' he said. I told him as much as I thought he needed to know. When I finished I said, ''You better be telling me the truth.''

Desmond Akeem Powell said, ''You also, sir. You also.'' George Benson had given way to Anita Baker. Desmond Akeem Powell said, ''I loved her.'' I left him sitting there with that.

CHAPTER

25

CHARLIE said, "You still here?"

I swiveled the chair around. "No."

"Peter," he said. He pointed at me with the Dr. Grabow. "You may not have found all you were looking for. But you found more than anyone else would have."

"Thanks, Charlie."

"Peter."

"Charlie."

"Take your wife to dinner. If you don't get out of here soon, you'll have to watch Ken and Barbie get ready for the news."

Charlie walked away through the newsroom. I unlocked the deep drawer, bottom right. I took it all out: Julie Samson's transcript. Scalia's transcript. Sara Hildreth's phone bill. An ashtray from the Astor Bar. Matchbooks. American Express receipts. The locket.

I opened the locket again.

Matchbooks from Googie's and Gil's and 21.

Why did I keep thinking I had missed something?

The phone rang.

Jeannie.

"I'm leaving now."

"Me too."

I put the stuff back in the drawer. I thought, maybe you can't miss anything because there's nothing to miss. . . .

DINNER was at Antolotti's on Forty-ninth, between First and Second. Marty said he would bring his mystery woman to Antolotti's, where he was meeting Mr. and Mrs. Finley and Jimmy O'Rourke. The mystery woman turned out to be Lea Ballard. Marty's confession went like this: "I've asked her to wear my old Washington Senators cap, and she's accepted."

Actually, Marty wasn't wearing a cap. He had on a blue blazer and a pink buttoned-down shirt and khaki pants and regulation Weejun loafers. His beard was trimmed. His hair, which had been a combination of crewcut and normal cut before the male models made that fashion, looked freshly trimmed too.

I said to him, "I now know what you're going to look like buried." I said to Lea, "You're too old for him."

O'Rourke said, "Miss Ballard, I hope it's not too late, and I was a little embarrassed to tell you that night at my own restaurant, but I love you."

I had told Jeannie about Lea, just not about AA. She just kept looking from Marty to Lea, beaming like they'd brought her presents. "This is wonderful," Jeannie Bogardus Finley said, and smiled one of the year's ten best smiles.

I said to Marty Pearl, "The first night you taunted me with a date, I was with Lea, we went to Knickerbocker's to wait for Michael Scalia."

"I figured if he was coming, he'd come before ten, and if he did come, you wouldn't let her stick around, because you like to play Travis McGee the lone wolf," Marty said. He ate one of the little pizzas Sonny Antolotti sends over to regulars as an appetizer. "We went to a ten o'clock show that night too, at the Baronet. We lucked into a sneak of the new Polanski movie. Whichamacallit's in it, Indiana Jones."

Lea said, "Harrison Ford."

"The talent is always the last to know," I said.

Jeannie said, "Professionally, personally, the whole ball of wax."

O'Rourke said to Lea, "You sure you don't just want to adopt him?"

I waved to George, our waiter, for menus. "This is going to be like *All About Eve*, isn't it, Marty? I take this girl in, I give her a shot in television, in about twenty minutes the show is going to be *The Ballard Report*, and I'm back in newspapers, covering the governor in Albany."

Marty said, "But there isn't anyone at the table who doesn't think you have a couple of good, productive years left."

"And I'll always be grateful to you, really," Lea said, patting my hand.

Jeannie clapped her hands together. "Everyone is going to be funnier than Peter tonight. I really am having a wonderful time."

O'Rourke wanted to know all about the Samson story. We told him while we all ate like fools. O'Rourke said, "But who killed the hooker girl in Douglaston?" and Lea told him Scalia's theory about that. O'Rourke said to Jeannie, "Who got into your guys' apartment?" I said, "We don't know. Scalia said that maybe Julie Samson was seeing one of the johns, he found out I was nosing around, and wanted to see if he could find out if I had anything, or scare me off."

"Golly, that always works with you," O'Rourke said. He checked his watch. The schoolteacher from Tenafly was meeting him at O'Rourkes after dinner; the rest of us were going to a ten o'clock movie down at the Cinema Village, *Johnny Come Lately* with James Cagney. "And you think these are the same guys who beat you up, scribe?"

"One was the same."

Marty said, "Sometimes you can't tie everything up with a ribbon, sport. Sometimes you take what you know, and that's all. You get one of the girls to back up Scalia, and you've got a hell of a story."

"I want all of it. Maybe Scalia had a way of sneaking out of the building that night. Maybe he really did kill Sara."

"If he did, Monaco will find out. Didn't he say the other

day, he had a boot print, something like that, and some skin under her fingernails?''

"Yeah."

"Besides, the escort service is the story.''

I said to Marty, "You feel like you know for sure why Julie did it? 'Cause she hated her father? Is that it? You think Sara was Scalia's partner for sure?''

He said, "You don't?''

"For all the things that aren't neat, that is pretty neat, her being dead and all. I think there's somebody out there we should know about that we didn't get to yet who could make me feel a lot happier than I do now.''

Jeannie said, "Do you know how much you're starting to sound like Delores?''

Sonny Antolotti came over to buy everyone an after-dinner drink. Marty and Lea had Perriers, I had coffee, Jeannie and O'Rourke ordered Amaretto. Sonny was a round man with a thin black-and-gray mustache and fat cheeks and his family had quietly run one of the best Italian restaurants in New York for thirty years. Sonny had branched out from pasta into thoroughbred racing. When he came over to the table, he always wanted to talk about the Mets or his horses, and this time he started in about how he had one running over at the Meadowlands tonight, his wife was over there having dinner with friends at that overpriced Pegasus, he didn't know how they could get away with charging prices like that at a racetrack, did we?, waiting for the seventh race, probably going to pick up the dinner check for everyone if the horse, named Sonny's Shine, won the damn race.

Sonny said, "Sonny's Shine wins, it may end up costing me money, of course.''

I looked at Sonny and said, "Of course.''

I said to Jeannie, "Would you guys mind going to the movies without me?''

She looked at me with her own Jeannie version of white lights.

"What's up? Something's up, isn't it? You have that look like something's up.''

I said, "I'm just going to go over to the station for a while, do some work. We're only gonna have a couple of days to turn this thing over if we want to put it on Thursday. I'm fine, really, I'm just not very good company tonight. I took a quick look at the tapes this afternoon. I keep thinking there's something in there that's not right. I'll try not to be too late." I kissed her lightly on the lips. "You know I must be in a lousy mood to miss a movie date with you, honey girl."

Marty said, "You want me to go with you?"

"No, I'm fine, really. Dwan said he was going to be in tonight, I just want to go through some of the tape with him. I'll go through it, then I'll know for sure that I'm crazy."

O'Rourke sipped his Amaretto. "The talent is always the last to know," he said.

THEY were finishing up the seven o'clock news when I got to my office. Ken and Barbie had closed with a feature about one of the captains of the Circle Line boats who sang opera. Dwan was in the control room. I poked my head in and said, "What happened to your Grace Jones cut?"

"I am going for the Michael Jordan close-to-the-skull very clean look for the summer," he said.

He was prettier than Grace, tall as Michael, wearing white slacks and some expensive white V-necked sweater that was supposed to look like a tennis sweater but probably cost five times as much, standing at ease behind the news director, because Dwan Bagley was always at ease.

I said, "Don't leave right away, okay?"

"Shit fire," he said, eyes narrowing. "You're doing this to me, aren't you?"

"It's nothing practically."

"Don't do this to me. You got that work-late look to you. I got a date. I got a fine date. Maxine. We are going to The Tunnel. Please do not do this to me. It is my first time to The Tunnel. You are my friend. I am your friend. We are brothers. We are part of the great rainbow coalition. We be the human experiment."

"The be stuff has never really worked with you, has it, DC? I think it's because you're too spiffy." I grinned. "It'll just be a couple of things on the stuff we brought in."

Dwan said, "Shit fire."

"Dwan?"

"What?"

"Lose shit fire."

I got a cup of coffee from the newsroom, went into my office, turned on the light, turned the radio to WNEW, heard Tony Bennett singing "I Wanna Be Around." Turned down the volume to where it was background music. Sat down. Unlocked the deep drawer, took it all out again, spread it in front of me on the desk.

Again.

Ferragamo box with the money in it.

Sara Hildreth's phone bill.

Matchbook covers and receipts and ashtray and locket.

And Julie Samson's transcript.

Michael Scalia's transcript.

Out loud I said, "So you did miss something, old Finley. Now what else?"

I remembered my wallet. I took out the key, and with it Jeannie's note, which I had forgotten. I opened the note and smiled. Before the Michael Scalia interview she had written, "Strumpets, harlots, courtesans. All of the above."

I went back into the drawer and came out with the emergency pack of Marlboros I had left in there, unwrapped the pack, lit one with a match from one of the books in front of me. I called 800 information, got the number I needed, said to the woman who answered, "This is Detective Monaco, Hundred-and-eleventh Precinct, Bayside Queens."

When I hung up, I started reading the transcripts again.

"YOU win the scavenger hunt?"

Dwan was standing in the doorway.

I motioned him over, handed him the first sheet of Sara Hildreth's long distance calls, took the second one for myself. "Start calling," I said. "You sit over there, use the two-four line. I'll use two-six. Anybody answers, give me a wave, I'll get on."

The fourth number on his sheet, Dwan waved.

* * *

TAPE room. Little after midnight.

I said, "Go back."

Dwan said, "How many times you gonna look at this?"

"There's something in there that doesn't fit. It's coming at me like it's out of sequence, I know it is."

He rewound the tape. The sound raced backward, made the funny squeaking noises of voices in reverse. I sipped cold coffee. I wanted another Marlboro, but I had already smoked three.

"Okay here? You've seen this one ten times."

"Go ahead."

Dwan started the tape forward.

There it was.

I said to the screen, "I didn't tell you that. So how did you know that?"

"YOU'RE shitting me?" Dwan said when I got back. "It worked?"

It was two in the morning.

"Worked. A guy deserves to get lucky once in a while."

"It doesn't mean anything by itself. You know that, right, Mr. PF Flyer?"

"Sure. It's just one more thing. I didn't even need it, actually. But it didn't surprise me."

"So now you're going back?"

"I am."

"You're seriously going to do this?"

"I am seriously going to do this."

"And you're going to sleep there?"

"I'm into ambush journalism. You saw the thing with young Lettie."

"You understand that you're going to have an hour, tops, once you start. You understand that too."

"You don't have to tell me, coach. I'm doing it for our school. I'm doing it for State."

"And you don't want me to call Marty?"

"If Marty's there, it doesn't work as well, I don't think. I called Jeannie, told her."

"She love the idea?"

I said, "Not the way she loves shopping, exactly."

CHAPTER
26

THERE was a transistor radio. I listened to an all-night sports talk show on what they kept advertising as "the world's first twenty-four-hour sports radio station." WFAN. I knew it because it was the Mets station. The callers identified themselves as Bruce from Flushing and Jerry from the Bronx and John from Hackensack. Some of them tried to stump the host with trivia questions. The host tried to act like he knew everything, but he didn't know that Reggie Smith was at second base for the Red Sox on Opening Day in 1967, not center, because Mike Andrews was hurt when the season started.

I thought about calling.

"Steve, hi, this is Peter from the Village."

"Go ahead, Peter from the Village."

"Listen, are you still giving away those Yankee-Red Sox tickets if I can answer the question correctly . . ."

There was a Mr. Coffee, and a can of Maxwell House in the refrigerator. I couldn't find filters so I used a napkin. When the door opened: Good morning, sleepyhead. Look, I've already got the coffee on. At five-thirty, I switched to WNBC and Imus and sipped coffee that tasted like it had been filtered through a napkin, or a dog, and picked up a book. *Julius Caesar*. Page One. Marullus: "But what trade art thou? Answer me directly." And the commoner, the cobbler guy, says, "A trade, sir, that I hope I may use with a safe conscience, which is indeed, sir, a mender of bad soles."

I thought, bad soles for you, pal. Bad souls for me.

I made myself another cup of coffee at seven-thirty. Imus was interviewing Larry Kenney, one of his regulars, doing a perfect Richard Nixon. I called Monaco, told him what I thought I had, asked him if I could play it my way. He said, "If I say no, what?" I said, "I won't tell you where I am." He said, "In that case, I accept your proposal." I told him the rest of the proposal.

At a few minutes after nine, I heard the key in the door. I had locked the door back up. Make everything seem normal.

Now just push the right button, noble tradesman.

I came around to the visitor's side of the desk, just stood there, facing the door.

He walked in, saw me, started to smile, stuffed the whole thing back inside his mouth. Without looking, he shut the door behind him.

Finally said, "How?"

I said, "Julie's key, Gus."

CHAPTER
27

I THOUGHT, Now just sit.

Gus Dancy had a stack of newspapers under his arm, the *Racing Form* on top. He dropped them on the couch, put his nose up in the air like he smelled something, looked over at the coffee machine.

"What did you use for a filter?"

"Napkin."

"Mind if I join you?"

"Suit yourself."

Sit yourself.

He poured coffee into a white mug that had TEACHER written in black letters. And sat down behind his desk. Augustus Dancy, my man, trying to play it cool in blue jeans, dark blue shirt, a tie a shade lighter than the shirt, and old motorcycle boots. He reached into the breast pocket of the shirt, got his Camels, lit one.

"What is this all about, old Finley? You say you used a key of Julie's to get into my office?"

I said, "I didn't need the key, Gus. The key just saved me time. If the key hadn't worked, and I had no way of knowing it was going to, I would have gotten into the office anyway.

Like O'Rourke and I did that time Hanrahan tried to lock us out of *The Square Deal*. You remember?''

''You gave Mr. O'Rourke credit for picking the lock that time, as I recall. Who would have done it this time, if I may ask?''

''Dwan Chandler from Channel A. Misspent youth, way uptown. Way, way uptown. He could get into the altar at St. Patrick's during High Mass.''

Get to it, Finley.

He said, ''You were looking for something?''

''Lots of things. Maybe my past, Gus. Maybe yours.''

''I don't follow.''

''I talked to Michael Scalia yesterday. He told me about Extra Credits, he told me about Julie and Sara and Lettie. He told me Sara was his partner. On camera and everything.''

Now he looked old.

''Extra Credits?''

''You never heard of it?''

''Old Finley, I am thoroughly confused.'' He blew some smoke at the ceiling. He had cut himself shaving. There was still a small piece of tissue paper stuck about an inch below his left ear.

''You're a liar. Good liar up until now, I'll give you that. But bad liar now. Definitely. Scalia doesn't have an excuse, lying's all he knows. I'm more interested in you. The guy who always talked about the truth. Who was that Yale president, Gus, the one you always quoted to us?''

''I'm sorry?''

''C'mon, you remember: 'We seek the truth, and will endure the consequences.' ''

''Seymour. Charles Seymour. He was there in the forties.''

''Damn, we liked that one so much we made it the motto of the damn *Square Deal*, like all the news that's fit to print. What are you fit for, Gus, you piece of garbage?''

He started to get out of the chair.

I said, ''Sit, Gus. I mean it. You just sit.'' He did. ''Sara Hildreth wasn't the partner at all, was she? It was you all along, Gus. You were the partner, you were Julie's new boy-friend, you killed Sara Hildreth. What we're going to talk about is why."

Dancy said, "I thought you gave up drugs long ago, Peter." Old Finley, that was gone, probably for good. "And you said you were never involved in the hallucinogens in the first place."

I stood up, came around to the back of my chair, leaned on the back of it. "You know what touched it off? This is actually pretty funny. A goddamned receipt from Pegasus. I found it with these other receipts from Saks and Tiffany's and like that, so I just assumed it was a store, no big deal, not even worth following up on. But it's not a store, is it, Gus? It's a restaurant at the Meadowlands. What did you call the Meadowlands, Gus? Home away from home? Said you eat there all the time, right?"

He watched me and smoked. "It helps me beat the rush hour traffic, and the food is surprisingly good. That's it?"

"Patience. So I called American Express, and I asked them to pull her record. And they did, finally, when the files reminded everybody she was dead, her father had closed the account. And you know what I found, Gus? Well, you probably do fucking know." I slammed both hands on the back of the chair. "Don't you?"

Dancy said, "She went there about once a week."

"Very good. Gold star for the professor. Tonight I'll go over to the Pegasus restaurant at the Meadowlands, and show the maitre d' a picture of the dead girl and a picture of the professor, and I'll bet he tells me the same thing."

"There is that possibility."

I put two fingers together, and he flipped me a cigarette. I lit it with Julie Samson's matchbook from the Astor Bar. "So now I had more of a connection between Julie Samson and Gus Dancy than Contemporary Bullshit. So I went back and looked at all the tape we'd shot. Had to look at a lot of it, Gus. Lot. But then I heard Gus Dancy saying, right before we started the interview under the arch, that he couldn't imagine how Julie Samson had accumulated ten thousand dollars. How'd you know it was ten thousand dollars, Gus?

And not five thousand, or twenty thousand, or a hundred thousand?''

"You told me."

"No, I never told you. And Marty didn't tell you, and neither did Lea or Jeannie. There's only one person who could've told you, because I told him, first time I met him. Know who that was, Gus?''

He got up to get more coffee. I waited until he sat back down. He said, "Go ahead, you're doing so well on your own."

"Michael Scalia, boy pimp. Your partner in a call girl ring running right out of your school. Washington Square U, give me a W. What does that make you, Gus? Pimp emeritus? Pimp Grand Master?''

"Scalia told you all this?''

"What, you don't think your buddy would give you up? You think there's an honor code for guys like you? See, that was another thing, Gus. You and Scalia. Wonderful mind for a hood, you said. Quite unique way of looking at things. A shark, old Finley."

"A shark."

"How'd you know so much about the shark? You said too much the first day I came to the office, didn't you?''

"It had been a bad couple of days at the track, I told you. A bit too much brandy to soothe the bettor's pain."

"I asked you if you knew him and you said yes, he took the same class as Julie. But I finally got around to thinking Gus Dancy might be full of shit and behind everything, I took a better look at Scalia's transcript, and you know what I found out? Damn, I found out he enrolled in the class all right, showed up one time, and withdrew. No grade next to Contemporary Bullshit. Just a 'W.' So how is it you know him so well, Gus?''

Dancy said, "You spin a good yarn, Peter. You always did. But the yarn is held together by yarn, is it not?''

I looked at my watch. Nine-twenty. And he wasn't helping.

"Was until about three this morning. I came down to Scalia's apartment, woke his ass up. I'd given him up to a cop from Bayside earlier in the evening, and the cop from Bayside scared the shit out of our boy. Scalia thought he had an airtight alibi for the night Sara Hildreth was killed. Had the doorman to back him up. But it turns out the doorman at the service entrance, Rico his name is, he broke down and admitted he was off getting laid, and Scalia could have gone and come back without anybody ever knowing. I told junior that wasn't half of it, I hadn't told Monaco yet that I had him, junior, on tape saying he already threatened to kill Sara Hildreth once because of Extra Credits. I told him to have a nice night's sleep, because in about four hours, he was gonna be up to his eyeballs in shit.''

I stopped. Wondered if I was lying as well to him as Scalia had lied to me.

Wondered if it was ever going to stop sounding like he was interviewing me.

I said, ''So what do you think happened next, Gus?''

''What happened next, Peter?''

''Well, sonofabitch, you can probably guess. He gave you up, Gus. He told me you were his partner, that you were sleeping with Julie, that you killed Sara Hildreth for the books, she'd run out of money and was trying to blackmail your ass, or she was going to tell me everything. She called O'Rourkes the night we had dinner there. You were downstairs. You brought the message back, didn't you? Said *she* said she'd had a change of heart.'' I stubbed out the Camel before I had to start smoking my fingers. ''It's over, Gus, is what we're talking about. The cop from Bayside doesn't have anything that can put Scalia out in Douglaston. But I bet he's got your skin, and your hair, sitting in a Baggie someplace, begging to find a match.''

He leaned back in his chair. Behind him, out the window, I could hear nails being pounded. The workmen had started about eight o'clock, finishing the stage in the middle of the park, the one to be used for graduation. Dancy put his head back, ran his hands through the long hair.

''What do you want, Peter?''

''I want to know why. Goddammit, Gus. I wanted to know what happened to you.''

He went over, filled up his mug with the last of the bad coffee, came back to his desk, opened a drawer on the left, pulled out a bottle of Hennessy, poured a dollop into the Teacher mug.

"You want to know." He drank out of the mug. "I sold grades," he said. "And I will tell you why, whether you care to understand or not." Another sip. "When I was busy here, before this . . . *place* forgot who I was, what I had been, I was able to keep the gambling under control. Like you would keep a drinking problem under control. But then, slowly, inexorably, I became the invisible man. Me. There goes old Gus Dancy, didn't he used to be something. Or somebody? They gave me what I least needed. Time. Soon it was not just the horses. I was betting on humans too. And doing quite badly. There were no articles anymore to balance the budget, no lectures. Near finals two years ago, I sold my first grade."

I thought of his speech at O'Rourkes. Thought: It must have been like confession, even though Jeannie and I didn't know. Bless me, students, for I have sinned . . .

I said, "You sold it to Sara Hildreth."

"I told you they do not burn for education anymore, Peter. They don't. They burn to find angles. I told her why I was doing it. Here I was, Professor Augustus Dancy, telling this little twit, about the pain of my *soul*!" He slammed down the mug, spilled coffee and Hennessy. "As I came to understand, she had quite a little business going for herself."

"And you had quite a little business going for yourself."

"I had my head above water. This was two years ago. I still had two lectures, two seminars. It was five hundred per grade. It financed my habit, and gave me a little cushion. But enough is never enough, is it? And once you have started selling yourself, it becomes easy."

"Scalia came to you."

"The girl, Miss Hildreth, told him I was involved. Apparently, she brokered a grade for him with somebody else. And Scalia asked me if I was tired of nickel-and-diming it, his words."

Scalia said he would turn Gus Dancy in if he didn't finance, at least at the start, Extra Credits. Sara Hildreth put up a little money. Gus Dancy got together four thousand dollars for a security deposit on the Village apartment they used as an office, two thousand for the first month's rent. And they were in business. I thought about Marty's material about the old Mickey Rooney-Judy Garland musicals:

Golly, the Professor's got the rent money.

And Mike can get the girls.

Let's put the hookers out . . . *right here*!

"Scalia ran the business. I cashed the checks. I told him one time, he should have stayed in my class, he would not have had to buy his A. All he needed to do was put down on paper the workings of Extra Credits. It would have been perfect for Contemporary Thought. He would have been my best student." He looked at me with vacant eyes. "Don't you see how funny that is, Peter?"

The business began to fall apart, because of the girls' fears about disease; Scalia had been telling the truth there. Gus Dancy began seeing Julie Samson; the two of them drifted into an affair, two sad, bruised people. I asked about Pegasus. One night a week, they would go to the track, it would be her treat, she insisted.

"Why the . . . how could you let her keep hooking?"

"I could not stop her," he said. "It was all about her father. It was a weapon against him. I said to her one time, 'If this is about him, why don't you tell him?' It was about a month before she died. She said, 'In due time.' "

I said, "Back up. Why did you kill Sara Hildreth?"

He looked at me, a long look, like it went all the way back.

"You are telling the truth about the evidence in the Baggie?"

"Yes."

"It is indeed over then."

"The cop's name is Monaco. I'm sure he's outside waiting for us by now."

"All right then." He sighed. "She had run out of money. Scalia had scared her off, of course. She couldn't do anything to him, she'd tried to threaten him with the books and he wasn't having any of it. But she had taken the books with her when she left. They were quite detailed. Names and dates and places. And checks with my name on them. She offered to sell them back to me.''

''Or else *she* would turn you in?''

''I demurred. She said she would go to you. At O'Rourkes that night, I found I was running out of time. She called looking for you, told O'Rourke to tell you she had had a change of heart, and for you to call her at work. I told him I would relay the message. Of course, I didn't. *I* called her, set up a meeting. Said I wanted to talk. I told her it would take me a few days to get together that kind of money . . .''

''How much?''

''Ten thousand. And the little bitch began to taunt me, taunt me down there by the water, saying she was tired of waiting, that by the next day, if she didn't have the money, what was left of my good name, which is all I had left, would be gone too. And my good name is what it had all been about, Peter. You can see that, can't you?''

''You killed her?''

Dead voice. ''Yes.''

''And searched her room until you found the books.''

''Searched her apartment and found the apartment had been searched.''

''Scalia?''

''He had gone out the same night, while she was at Patrick's Pub. And here is the hilarious part, Peter, the part where passions had spun the plot, as Meredith said. Now he had the books. But they were for sale. For fifteen thousand. A one-time, one-week offer, he said.''

Fifteen from Channel A, fifteen from Gus Dancy.

''You paid?''

''I thought about the alternative, but decided one killing was more than enough. I had killed because of money, and in killing because of money, it had cost me more. True poetic justice, don't you think?''

''Maybe you should have killed me, Gus.''

''How could I, old Finley? Don't you see? You were my past. And it was all I had left.''

I looked at my watch. Nine-fifty.

I said, "I need to know a couple more things."

He told me the rest of it.

"YOU ready?" I was at the window. I could see Monaco leaning against his car on the street. Ten oh-five. I would come back later for the Camcorder I had hidden in the stacks of books, aimed at Gus Dancy's chair. Camcorder with an hour of tape to it.

I had no way of knowing how it would go with him. I had to make sure.

"Gus. You ready?"

Gus Dancy said, "Yes." We walked to the door. He said, "Wait, my cigarettes," went back to his desk. We walked down the stairs and out into the morning.

Gus Dancy said, "Detective, can I ask for your indulgence?"

Monaco looked at him, then me. "Sure."

"Could you pull around to the arch, while old Finley and I walk across the park one last time? For old times' sake?"

Monaco said to me, "Okay with you?"

"For old times' sake."

And so we walked past the petanque courts and moved past Garibaldi and Gus looked at the stage that was all-the-way built now and said, "One more stage," and left me near Garibaldi as he walked up the stairs, and it was too late by the time I saw he was pulling the gun out of the pocket where the cigarettes were supposed to be, and nobody heard my yell in Washington Square Park because the sound of the gun was the only thing anyone heard.

CHAPTER

28

JEANNIE rode with me in the red Taurus we had rented. Marty and Lea followed in the van. We got lost once going through the town of New Canaan, but then I asked at a Sunoco station across from the train station, and a kid in a New Canaan Rams sweatshirt told me how to get to Route 124. He said once we got to 124, stay on it, we'd cross the state line without knowing it.

We went out of town, up a hill, past a beautiful white-steepled country church, past The Maple Inn, past The Roger Sherman Inn. On the radio Whitney Houston sang "All at Once."

Jeannie had been quiet since we left the hospital, so had I. The land opened up on both sides of us on 124, and down a hill, past a fenced-in place for horses, I could see a lake.

I said, "Jamie. The funny thing is, he mentioned her when I talked to him."

Jeannie said, "It goes all the way back to her, doesn't it?"

"It goes back to him. The sonofabitch."

I passed a truck that had "Pennington Roofing, New Canaan" on the side. Jeannie sighed. "My God, Peter, have you ever seen anything as sad? That beautiful girl, lost in her own world. But the doctor is right, of course. With two of them going through it, it would be rare for them to deal with it the same way, emotionally. One acts in, one acts out.''

"If she had turned it all outward, being the older one, Julie could have ended up withdrawing completely?''

"Peter, it's like the doctor said, 'Put both of them in a Waring blender, you'd have two of the most powerful aspects of self-destructive behavior.' Julie wanted to hurt her father. The sister wanted to hurt herself.''

"I got that part. The part I didn't get was the doctor saying if Julie had been a man, she might have turned to rape.''

"It all makes sense, Peter. If you think about it, prostitution can be seen as an act of revenge against men. Sublime violence. Julie finally had power over men. What she couldn't see, until the end perhaps, was that in trying to hurt them, she was only acting with hatred toward herself.''

"The doctors must have known the business about the accident was a lie.''

"Not necessarily. They knew it had been a trauma of some kind, they just didn't know what kind. Weren't you listening? Listening is one of your good things usually. Something triggers this kind of emotional response. The child begins withdrawing. In her case, it was a drunken, abusive father, beating a helpless little girl. But it *could* have been the accident, losing the mother that day. She would probably stop eating at first, something like that, spend more time in her room, finally lose interest in life altogether, and cease communications entirely. It is a form of catatonia, but it's not really catatonia. It is a rage that cannot be expressed, basically.''

"Why wouldn't Julie have told them sooner than what turned out to be her last visit?''

Jeannie said, "Because she was still afraid of him. As much as she was trying to hurt him back with her behavior, first the small rebellions of going off to school when he didn't want her to, then with Scalia, finally the prostitution, she was still the little girl who was terrified of him. She only broke loose when she decided to kill herself.''

I said, "Thank God she confided in Gus.''

''But what was he trying to do with Lea and you? Even me?''

''When Julie died, he must have figured he was home free. Maybe he was afraid I would find out. But it was so clumsy, unless he was looking for something. It's what we're here to find out, anyway.''

Jeannie said, ''Once a bully, always a bully.''

''Sixteen,'' I said to Jeannie. ''She's been in there since she was sixteen.''

The Scotts Corner shopping mall was on our right, a sign that said Gilmore Designs, a Texaco station, Albano Electronics. It was a busy Saturday afternoon in the late spring, people on the streets of the little town, cars lined up on both sides. The line at The Italian Deli stretched out the door. The Pound Ridge Fire Department was next door to The Italian Deli. Jeannie read the map, because I could make more sense of *The National Review* than a road map. We took the first left after we got through town, then a right on Hemlock Hill road. Arthur Samson's home turned out to be fourth on the left.

I said, ''You have the cassette?''

''For the fortieth time, Toots, I have the cassette.''

The driveway snaked up a hill and around a garden to the front of the house. A garage big enough for three was on the right. A stretch Mercedes was being washed gently by hand. The short man washing it stopped when he noticed our humble one-car, one-van caravan.

Jeannie said, ''My God, Peter, that's him. The man.''

Jeannie's world was divided into loved ones, acquaintances, other women, and The Man. But I knew which one she meant.

''Really?''

''Really.''

I said, ''If you think of it, why not? Samson probably doesn't know a lot of guys named Cheech.''

I got out of the car and walked over to the Mercedes. Marty was coming from the van.

Shorty still had a bit of a scab on his cheek, from where Jeannie scratched him. I said, ''You're shitting me. You're

Samson's idea of muscle? Where'd he get you, FAO Schwartz?''

He started to make a move toward a wrench that was lying next to the Mercedes. When he bent down, Marty Pearl grabbed him by his hair, straightened him up, looked at me, asked, ''You mind?'' I said, ''Be my guest.'' Marty back-handed him across the face and into the bucket of water he was using on the Mercedes.

Marty knelt down next to him. ''I guess my friend probably told you it was a bad idea to hit Mrs. Finley.'' Then backhanded him again.

Marty said, ''What do we do with him?''

I opened the trunk. There was his cute little limo driver's cap. ''We'll put him in here till we're done with daddy.''

We did that.

THE house was a beauty. It had been a barn once, but now it had grown by at least a couple of additions, and the outside was brick, top to bottom, end to end, ivy growing on the walls and around white shutters. Off to the left was a green-house and beyond the greenhouse, down a hill, was what looked like a Har-Tru tennis court, a ball machine standing guard in the corner.

The front door was open. The four of us walked in. I told Marty to forget the camera. If anything, we had come to watch pictures, not take them.

In the foyer I grinned at Jeannie.

I called out, ''Margaret, I'm hoooooommmme.''

Arthur Samson came walking through a sliding glass door at the other end of the foyer. The pool entrance. He was wearing a white golf shirt, white sweater, lemon-colored slacks, white Avia sneakers. He was also carrying a glass filled with ice, a clear liquid, and olives.

He said to me, ''I beg your pardon.''

''Hello, Arthur. This is my wife, Jeannie. Your man beat her up.''

Jeannie said, ''Hi, Arthur.''

I said, ''This is Lea Ballard. You remember her from your office. Your man broke into her room. And this very big man''—I nodded at Marty—''is Marty Pearl. He just stuffed your man into the trunk of your Mercedes.''

Arthur Samson said, ''I'm calling the police.'' But didn't make any moves toward a phone. He could have said he was calling a United Nations Peacekeeping Force.

I said, ''Shut up, Arthur. We have been to see your daughter Jamie at the Silver Hill Foundation Psychiatric Hospital in New Canaan. We have what amounts to a deathbed statement from the late Professor Gus Dancy, in which he tells of Julie telling *him* before she died about how both she and her sister were abused by you throughout their adolescence, perhaps even sexually. My wife will identify your driver as the man who broke into our apartment and struck her. You want to see the cassette, Arthur?''

''No.''

He walked over to what looked like an antique country cupboard, painted blue, set his drink down, walked over to where we all stood.

''What do you want from me?'' he said.

''I want to know what you were trying to do with me. Hell, all of us. What were you looking for?''

He looked at me with those sad red drinker's eyes in the early afternoon. ''Can we talk about this? Would you like to come in and sit down?''

He wasn't a corporate bruiser anymore.

''Not really,'' I said. ''Like I said, the last part of it is what you wanted from me.''

''I really didn't know what I wanted at first, other than I didn't need you around, poking into Julie's life. I was looking for anything that would tie Julie to the Extra Credits business, or to Jamie. I had the appointment from the mayor; it was mine. It was to be announced sometime this week. I didn't want you mucking it up for me. I thought you, or Miss Ballard, might have something, and not know you had it.''

Lea said, ''Wait a minute. You *knew* about Extra Credits?''

''Didn't you ever wonder why there wasn't a note, Miss Ballard? Mr. Finley? Well, there was a note. It came in the mail the day after her death. And it told of . . . what her life had become. I will spare you the details, but it was what you would have expected, knowing what you now know. She said it was her way of hitting me back. For her, and for Jamie."

I said, "What you said when Lea and I first came to your office, it was all just a show?" Samson said, "Not all. But a lot." Then no one said anything. Arthur Samson went back and picked up the martini, drank some, came back to where we stood. Group of five, chatting it up at a cocktail party at the Samsons' in Pound Ridge.

"I frankly figured I was still in the clear. The mayor's people had investigated me, of course. They knew of Jamie, but they were convinced, like everyone has always been convinced, by the story about the accident. She was in the car that day. So was her brother. Julie's death made me a tragic figure, but not, um, unappointable. And then you and Miss Ballard came along. I kept waiting for Scalia to step forward, ask for money, but he never did. I knew you were chasing him, even if you didn't know it. I just wanted to . . . *hinder* you in any way I could. So I got John involved. When you called me the other night, said you were going back to Julie's room, I told John to convince you in the strongest possible terms to let it go. Short of killing you, I didn't know what else to do."

"Do you know why she kept ten thousand dollars in her room?"

He put a finger into his glass, stirred the ice around, said, "She liked to bring her sister presents. She said someone had to."

I said, "We're out of here."

Arthur Samson said, "What are you going to do?"

I turned around at the door, "A television show. I don't know exactly what it's going to look like. But here's what I do know: You're not going to work for the mayor, Arthur."

Marty and Lea were outside, getting the Betacam out of the van. Jeannie and I were in the doorway. Jeannie said to me, "You hear any remorse there?" I said, "Only about losing that job." She said, "Righto." She walked back across the foyer and wound up from behind her back and slapped Arthur Samson hard as she could across the face with her right hand, knocking him backward, glass falling to the marble floor and shattering.

"It feels something like that," she said to him.

Jeannie Bogardus Finley turned around and walked back to me and said, "We're done here, sport."

About the Author

At the *New York Daily News*, The *National*, and *Esquire*, Mike Lupica has become one of the best-known sports columnists in the United States. In 1986, he was named National Sports Columnist of the Year by the National Headliners Association. He is also a commentator for ESPN's coverage of major league baseball. *Extra Credits* is his second Peter Finley mystery. The first, *Dead Air*, was nominated for an Edgar Award as Best First Mystery, and became the CBS movie, *Money, Power and Murder*, for which Lupica wrote the teleplay. He lives with his wife, Taylor, and their two sons in New Canaan, Connecticut, and Jupiter, Florida.

If
"A.P.B." "B.O.L.O."'d You
Over, Then
"A.K.A." Will Make You
"D.O.A." Just ask
DAVE PEDNEAU...
O.K.?